Rawson stopped and looked back into the depths. "I'm leavin', gents," he said coldly.

"You leave us here like this and we'll come after you. That's a promise. We'll find you and kill you—slow."

"You'll have to get free first," Rawson taunted.

"We will."

Rawson smiled. "You won't get far without horses."

"Damn you! Damn your miserable hide! We'll find you if we have to ride through the gates of hell to do it!"

Rawson turned his back on them and stepped into the sunshine. "That's just what you'll have to do."

OTHER BOOKS BY JAKE LOGAN

JAKE LOGAN

SLOCUM AND THE
LOST DUTCHMAN MINE

BERKLEY BOOKS, NEW YORK

SLOCUM AND THE LOST DUTCHMAN MINE

A Berkley Book / published by arrangement with
the author

PRINTING HISTORY
Berkley edition / January 1984

ISBN: 0-425-06744-0

A BERKLEY BOOK ® TM 757,375
Berkley Books are published by The Berkley Publishing Group,
200 Madison Avenue, New York, N.Y. 10016.
The name "BERKLEY" and the stylized "B" with design are
trademarks belonging to Berkley Publishing Corporation.

PRINTED IN THE UNITED STATES OF AMERICA

SLOCUM AND THE
LOST DUTCHMAN MINE

1

Peering into the blistering, sun-blasted canyon, Slocum swore. He was almost certain he had seen the son of a bitch, but all he saw now were sheer rock walls and parched brush shimmering in the heat. He returned his Winchester to its scabbard and took up his reins again, letting his big dun pick its way down the rocky trail that led to the canyon mouth.

The sun sat on him like a hot fist. Having followed his quarry deep into the Superstition Mountains, Slocum had lost him the evening before; and since that time all he had seen moving in this rocky inferno were a few scorpions and lizards, and overhead one or two buzzards, drifting lazily in the hot air like burnt-out cinders.

Slocum's horse shook its head unhappily and let its head droop a few inches lower. Slocum did not blame his mount. Hell's bells, he didn't feel so great himself. His canteen was as dry as a pharaoh's tomb and neither horse nor rider had seen fresh water since that morning.

John Slocum was riding deeper into this blistering wasteland to recapture a man he thought he had tucked away for life: Tate Rawson. Two weeks before, Tate had killed a guard while breaking out of Yuma Prison. As soon as Slocum had heard the news, he had assigned himself the task of going after the grim son of a bitch a second time.

Tate Rawson was a homicidal maniac, a bank robber who liked to take hostages, then leave pieces of them on the trail behind him. One of the hostages he had used in this fashion had been an old friend of Slocum's, and when Slocum had looked down into Tim Farber's coffin and seen what Tate had done to him, Slocum had vowed to bring Tate Rawson in. After spending the best part of a blistering summer tracking down the bastard three years before, Slocum had finally brought him in, trussed like a turkey and slung over his pommel. Instead of hanging the killer, however, a mealymouthed judge had given Rawson life in Yuma Prison. But now Tate Rawson was out again, with the fresh blood of another human on his black soul.

This time, Slocum promised himself, he would not return Tate Rawson to Yuma alive. He'd return once again with Rawson slung over his pommel, but when Tate was cut down, the cell they gave him would be six feet deep and the walls would be of rough-cut pine.

Damn it! What was that now?

Slocum reined in and peered through the hammering heat. Far above him on the rim of a canyon was a girl. Her hair was Indian black, her green spangled dress so torn there was little left of it. And she was waving frantically, desperately to him. Was this some trick of Tate Rawson's? Had the son of a bitch taken her as hostage?

He was raising his arm to wave back to her so she would know he had seen her when a man came up to her from behind and dragged her from sight. Slocum swore. At this distance he could not be certain the man was Tate Rawson, but it well might be. A moment before Slocum had thought Tate was below him in the canyon, but whatever it was he had seen—or thought he had seen—it was more than likely this cursed heat playing tricks on him.

Slocum turned his horse off the slope and urged it up a narrow game trail that led to the canyon rim.

In the canyon below, Tate bared his teeth in sudden perplexity. That bastard Slocum was turning off the trail leading into the canyon. He was heading out of sight.

Tate had crowded himself into a narrow cleft behind a huge boulder beside the trail. A horse he had stolen had given out a week before and all he had now for weaponry was that guard's Colt and two rounds. By this time he was half mad with thirst and hunger. He had planned to blast Slocum from his saddle, take what jerky he might have, and then drink deep from the canteen slung over his saddle horn. After that he would mount Slocum's horse and ride out of this hell into the cool north country, maybe even into Canada. The moment he had realized Slocum was tailing him, he had looked upon the big hard-nosed bastard's arrival as a Godsend.

Damn! What could have turned Slocum?

Slumping to the ground, Tate gazed up through slitted eyes at the canyon rim. Just before he turned off the trail, Slocum had glanced in that direction and started to wave. What had he seen?

Tate closed his eyes and sank back into the cool shadow of the boulder. He had to keep going. He had to find out what Slocum was up to. But not now, he told himself dimly. Later, when the sun went down; when he got some of his strength back.

Dimly, he heard his Colt clatter to the ground beside him as he fell into an exhausted sleep.

The girl's name was Topaz. There was more Apache blood in her than Spanish, but it was the Spanish side of her that gave her the long, willowy figure, the sharp, uncompromising nose, and the blue eyes. But all the rest of her—including her capacity to fight— was Apache.

As Shorty Bolin dragged her back down the trail, she kicked out at him again, and this time caught him a nasty crack in the shins. As the fellow bent with a cry, his hand grabbing for his shin, she raked a hooked claw of a hand down his face. Furious, he brought up his six-gun and cracked her on the side of the head. She went sprawling, coming down hard on the rocky trail.

When she made no effort to get up, Shorty figured the blow had knocked her out and he bent to sling her over his shoulder. She came awake on the instant, striking up at him like a rattlesnake. Her knee found his groin as her fists and elbows punished him about the face and head. Groaning, he backed up, aware that he had a loose wildcat on his hands. He needed help if he were going to bring her back to the mine in one piece.

"Slate!" he cried. "Slate!"

Continuing to pummel him furiously, Topaz tried to snatch the gun from his hand. When he pulled his gun hand back, she sank her bright white teeth into the skin just above his knuckles. With a howl, he dropped the weapon and stumbled back.

Topaz pounced on the Colt and was about to raise it when a long shadow fell over her. Before she could turn, Slate Cadey brought down the barrel of his own Colt onto her head. This time when the girl collapsed to the ground, she was truly unconscious.

"Give me a hand with her, Shorty," Slate said, the trace of a chuckle in his voice. "I would have helped you sooner, but I liked the way this wildcat came after you. Can you imagine what it's going to be like when we take our turns on her?"

Shorty glanced unhappily up at Slate. He was a chunky man, little more than five feet five inches tall, with short, yellowish hair and a round, freckled face burnt raw by the sun. His companion was a gray, balding fellow, with yellow broken teeth. For some reason he liked to smile.

"Sure I can imagine," said Shorty. "But I don't see how it will be much of a pleasure. Not the way she kicks and bites."

"Take it from me," said Slate, flashing his broken teeth at Shorty. "You will."

Slate took Topaz's head and shoulders, Shorty her feet, and with Shorty backing up carefully, they worked their way back down the narrow arroyo to the canyon floor.

This was not the same canyon Slocum had been riding toward when he caught sight of Topaz signaling him. It was another, longer, narrower canyon that ran parallel to it. And off this one ran still other canyons and steep-sided draws. This particular stretch of the Superstition Mountains was honeycombed with these serpentine canyons, many of which were hidden away so completely that once lost in their labyrinthine coils countless explorers and prospectors had disappeared completely, never to be found again—unless it was by the Apaches, who called these mountains sacred.

As soon as the two men reached the bottom they turned about and walked along the narrow canyon floor for nearly half a mile, the girl slung between them. At last, both men breathing heavily, black ribbons of sweat streaming down their faces and across their bared, blistered torsos, they reached a mine and entered it. Unceremoniously dumping the girl onto the ground, Slate tied her wrists behind her with rawhide, then bound her ankles together also. He was not careful as he worked, and Shorty saw how the rawhide cut into her sleek olive flesh.

"You're cuttin' her," he said.

"I know," Slate said. "She's gonna be damn anxious for us to let her loose once she wakes up again." Again Slate flashed that unpleasant smile at his partner. "And when she does, maybe the two of us can make a deal."

Topaz opened her eyes. They blazed up at Slate. "Never!" she cried. "Never will I deal with the likes of you!" She spat then, catching Slate on the cheek.

He stumbled quickly backward, wiping his face, his fanged mouth twisting into a snarl. "We'll see!" he said.

"You'll see what?" a voice demanded from the darkened mine shaft behind them.

Slate turned, recognizing the voice of Ben Stringfellow. Peering into the blackness of the mine shaft, Slate could see nothing.

"This here bitch is giving us trouble, Ben!" he cried into the shaft. "She's a real scorpion."

There was no reply, but two men came out of the mine shaft. The first was an old duffer, his white beard yellowed with tobacco juice, his eyes dim. He walked with an arthritic stoop. The man who came after him was Ben. He was considerably younger and was pushing the old man roughly ahead of him as he struggled toward the light. When he reached Slate and Shorty, he pushed the old man brutally to the floor of the shaft, causing him to strike the unyielding ground with a painful gasp.

"Any luck, Ben?" Slate asked hopefully. "We been here better than a week now."

"You don't need to tell me that," Ben Stringfellow

replied bitterly. Ben was as brown as a piece of raw-hide and just about as stringy. His age was difficult to determine. He had a gaunt, wrinkled face and long, gray, matted hair that ran down past his shoulders. "I know how damn long we been here."

"You think maybe we should pull out?" Slate asked.

"Maybe. After burying this old lying bastard."

"I say no," said Shorty.

"Why?" demanded Ben, turning on the smaller man.

"Because we came here for gold. I say we ought to stay until we find it," Shorty declared.

"Stay, then. All we seen so far is rock and fool's gold, and maybe a little copper. But no gold—not a trace!"

"He's holding out," said Shorty. "I know he is."

As he spoke, Shorty stepped forward and kicked the old man viciously in the side. "What about it, Blucher? Where's that Dutchman's gold? We been digging for a week now!"

Blucher groaned painfully and tried to sit up. Shorty kicked him again to hurry him along. The old man rolled over to face his tormentors.

"Leave me be!" he cried, "I'm hurt."

"You ain't hurt near as bad as you're gonna be," said Slate impatiently. "Where's that gold?"

"All I know is what the Dutchman told me!"

"We heard that before!"

"This is the place, I tell you. I remember that much. And you saw them gold nuggets the Dutchman left at the assay office. You know them nuggets're the real thing."

"They ain't real if we can't find them!" said the last man to emerge from the mine shaft.

The others turned to face the newcomer as he

emerged, blinking, into the brilliant sunlight.

This was Mat Wall, their leader. Of the four, Wall was the most desperate in appearance. As dirty and as lank as his three companions, he had a face that would scare a rebellious child into sainthood. The right side of it had been caved in years before by the plunging hoof of a runaway Percheron draft horse. Wall had no right cheekbone, and where his eye should have been there remained only a filthy, ragged black patch. Mat took a perverse pleasure in thrusting this broken visage of his close to the squeamish—the women he purchased for an evening's pleasure, especially. He liked to see them quail. And the moment they turned their heads or averted their eyes, he would reach out and snap them brutally around, then lift off his eye patch and force them to gaze long and hard into that gleaming, puckered hole that had once been an eye socket.

Striding past the others, Mat reached down and dragged the old man to his feet. Thrusting his ugly countenance within an inch of Blucher's, he snarled, "You been lying to us all along! There ain't no gold down there! It's all been played out long ago!"

"No!" gasped Blucher. "I told you! Jacob said there was another branch. He said it was in there! And just now we found it. You said it was too late to explore it, but that's where the gold is! It's up in there—great big nuggets, as big as your fist!"

"They damn well better be up there!" said Wall, flinging the old man back down.

Blucher struck the hard ground awkwardly, landing on his elbow. He cried out in sudden pain and began to rub his arm.

"Leave him alone!" cried the girl.

Mat turned his attention to Topaz, and what passed for a smile spread across his face. He walked closer to her, then hunkered down. "They got you trussed good and proper, I see. Maybe now you'll stay put." He slapped her hard. Standing up, he glanced at Slate. "How far did she get?" he asked.

"Far enough."

"I was the one caught her," said Shorty. "She had broken on top of the canyon and was waving to a rider below."

"She was *what?*"

"I told you, she was waving to some rider," said Shorty.

"Did he see her?" Wall demanded.

"I don't know. I was so busy trying to handle her, I couldn't tell. But he was a long way off and was heading the other way." Shorty shook his head and glanced down at Topaz. "She sure as hell put up a scrap. She near broke my shin."

Slate nodded confirmation. "When I came on them, she was getting ready to cut Shorty up into little pieces. She had his gun in her hand."

Ben swung back to look at Shorty, then grinned, shaking his head. "You better watch out for her, Shorty. She'll just eat you alive, she will—then spit you out to make room for dessert."

"I don't like it," said Mat. "If that rider saw her he might come moseying in this direction."

Ben looked thoughtfully down at the girl. "She would draw a man, at that."

"I say we truss Blucher up, too, then take a look," Mat went on. "I don't aim to share this gold with anyone else."

"If there *is* any gold," Ben growled.

"No sense arguing that now. Tie up Blucher, pronto."

There was no more discussion as Slate bent to tie the old prospector's hands behind his back.

Slocum was beginning to feel a little foolish. He had reached the rim of the canyon where he had seen the girl. But as soon as he came to the spot, he realized how difficult it would be to pinpoint the spot where the girl and Rawson—if it had been Rawson—were struggling.

Every landmark that had stood out so clearly from a distance now assumed a totally different aspect once he had pulled to a halt atop the rim. From where he sat his dun, steep-sided canyon walls dropped away on all sides. The entire wind-scoured land was surrounded by abrupt, vaulting peaks and the intimidating, shrouding brows of overhanging ledges. High above him, great boulders were perched precariously, waiting to be sent crashing down upon him. Some of the boulders were reddish in tint, others were gleaming blades of black basalt, as smooth as glass. Over it all hung the numbing, shriveling heat of damnation.

If there was a hell on earth, Slocum felt, this patch of real estate was it, and these frozen rock forms looming about him were the congealed souls of sinners in everlasting torment.

Slocum kept his dun moving in a direction that would take him to where he thought he had seen the man grab the girl. At last he reached the rim of a canyon. Dismounting, he looked for tracks. But it was all cap rock here and though he thought he caught the faint dusty pattern of footprints on the rock, he could not be sure.

He moved closer to the edge of the rim and peered over. Far below, flowing through the middle of the canyon, he saw the thin blue tracery of a stream. At once Slocum realized how much he and his mount needed that water. Reluctant though he was to abandon the search for Tate and his hostage, he decided he would have to find a way to the canyon floor and see to himself and his horse first. He could do nothing for the girl, and he certainly would not be any threat to Tate Rawson, if his bones and those of his mount were left to bleach in this hellish sun.

About a quarter of a mile farther on, Slocum found a narrow game trail that led from the rim and directed his horse onto it. About halfway down, the shale and talus under the dun's feet became so treacherous that he dismounted and led his horse the rest of the way. The scub pine on the floor of the canyon exuded a sharp, kerosene-like tang. Slocum was almost certain that if he struck one of his sulphur matches and flung it at a pine, the entire stand would explode into flame.

As Slocum led the dun toward the stream, the horse whinnied in anticipation. When he reached it, Slocum did not let the horse drink at once. Instead he dampened his bandanna and patted the horse's nose and mouth with it, squeezing it to let some of the water dribble into the animal's mouth. When he was sure the horse was ready for the water, he allowed it to drink. Then he went down on all fours beside the larger beast and drank from his cupped hands. After that, Slocum filled his hat and poured water over his head and down his neck. Jesus, but that felt good!

He filled his canteen, led the horse over to the cliffside where there was some shade, and off-saddled the dun. Peeling off the sweat-soaked saddle blanket, he spent a few minutes drying off the animal, then grooming it. The horse stood patiently as Slocum moved the stiff-bristled brush along its back. Occasionally the dun would flick its ears in contentment and nod its head, expressing its pleasure as a woman would, Slocum mused, if he soothed her in the same fashion.

There was a small patch of grass in the shade on the other side of the canyon. Slocum led the horse over to the spot and hobbled it. He had no more grain for his mount; the dun would simply have to subsist on grass for a while. Moving back across the canyon, Slocum poked carefully about with his rifle barrel to make sure there were no snakes hidden in the shadowy clefts—and no scorpions, either. Then he eased himself down with his back to the canyon wall and tried to figure his next move.

More than likely, when he found Rawson, he would find the girl as well. The thought of her as Tate's hostage was not pleasant to contemplate. He remembered how Rawson had dealt with hostages in the past. Still, this girl had looked healthy enough to appease Rawson's other appetites—for now, at least.

Now that he had had a chance to go over that scene once again in his mind, Slocum realized that there was still an outside chance that it was not Tate Rawson he had seen struggling with the girl. Slocum had gotten only the quickest glimpse of the man, but the man dragging the girl back from the rim had seemed a mite shorter and stockier than Tate Rawson, if that meant anything. Tate could have put on a lot of tallow sitting in a Yuma cell these past three years.

Slocum shook his head in frustration and cursed once again for having allowed himself to lose Rawson's trail the evening before. He had been so close to the man he could almost smell him. He should have realized that if he could smell Rawson, Rawson could smell him as well.

Slocum looked around him warily. The canyon seemed to have been struck dumb by the stupefying heat. The water in the stream was as still as a shaving mirror, the landscape as barren as the moon, with not even a bird song to break the awful, waiting silence. Slocum sighed. His belly full of water and his eyes burning from the sun, he found himself teetering on the brink of sleep. And for a moment he allowed himself to think it was safe for him to grab a little shut-eye.

But he heard something that alerted him instantly. It was the thin, rattling sound of a small avalanche of rock spilling to the canyon floor a few yards further down the canyon. Fully awake on the instant, Slocum got to his feet and levered a fresh round into the Winchester's firing chamber, then flattened himself against the rock wall.

He waited, but he saw and heard nothing.

The tiny avalanche had come to a halt, having deposited a mound of sand and gravel about a foot high on the canyon floor.

Slocum waited.

Across the canyon, the horse lifted its head from the grass and glanced up at the wall over Slocum's head, ears flicking nervously. Slocum stepped out from the wall and glanced up. A man was moving down a steep trail, a rifle in his hand. About twenty yards farther down, another man—the same fellow who had grabbed the girl—was also in the act of climbing down. All he was carrying was a Colt. They were caught in plain sight with little cover. It was almost too easy.

"Drop them weapons!" Slocum called.

Instead, the man with the rifle ducked behind an outcropping of rock and fired wildly down at Slocum. As the round exploded at his feet, Slocum aimed carefully and fired back up at him. He heard the man cry out and saw the rifle drop. It began to slide down the steep slope to the canyon floor. The other one brought up his Colt and fired also. The shot went wild, and Slocum levered swiftly and raised his rifle a second time.

Too late, he heard the sound of running feet behind him, and started to turn. Before he could make it, what felt like the canyon wall crashed down upon his skull.

His knees gave way and he sank unconscious to the ground.

Tate Rawson awoke from a heat-shriveling nightmare, sweat swimming on his body, his lips swollen, his mouth as dry as an old newspaper. He had heard shots; he was certain of it.

There it was again! Tate recognized the sound instantly. Three shots in all. He waited, but there was no more firing. The echoes died. The shots seemed to have come from another world, so dim had they been. He squinted in the direction from which he thought they had come. But how could he be sure he was looking in the right direction? The echoing rocks had taken the sound and played tricks with it, making it louder in some places, killing it in others.

What it meant was that he was not alone in this wilderness of rock and brush. Somewhere there were others like himself, perhaps as eager as he was to exchange fire with John Slocum. For all he knew, those shots he had just heard had cut down Slocum for good. The gunfire could well have come from the direction he had seen Slocum take when he veered away from the canyon entrance.

Tate pushed himself back and leaned wearily against the canyon wall. In doing so, he placed his hand down on the flat surface of a rock, immediately blistering the palm. He yanked his hand away. The rock moved, and he felt something clinging to the back of his hand. He looked down. It was a scorpion, its huge tail coiled over its back.

For a moment Tate froze in horror. Then, with a shriek, he jumped up, waving his hand wildly. He felt the scorpion pass close by his shoulder, heard it bounce off the wall, then strike his back. He flung himself about and started beating at his clothes. His feet dislodged a few boulders against the rock wall, and a rattler appeared and began to uncoil, its head peering up at him, its dry rattle filling the air with its warning.

Shrieking, Tate bolted away from the canyon wall and charged across the dry streambed. His foot sank in the soft sand and he went sprawling. When he looked up, he saw another scorpion, inches from his eyes. With a soul-shattering cry of sheer, overmastering terror, Tate plunged to his feet and raced off toward the gunfire he had heard earlier, his hair standing straight up on end, his mind teetering on the brink.

He was certain now that every venomous creature in this canyon was after him personally.

2

As soon as Slocum struck the ground, Mat began to kick him furiously. Finally Ben had to pull him off.

"We can use the son of a bitch," he said. "We can make him dig for us. Hold off! Hold off!"

Mat shook Ben off and ran a hand through his hair. His eye patch had slipped down when he began kicking Slocum and the hole in his face made Ben's stomach crawl. But Ben swallowed and dared not let himself look away.

"All right," Mat said, panting slightly. "We'll use him to dig for us. That's a good idea—a damn good idea. When we reach the gold, we'll need a big son of a bitch like this to haul out that heavy ore." He stepped back and, taking a deep breath, glanced over at the others. "How is Slate?"

Ben looked up and watched Shorty helping Slate pick his way down the rest of the almost sheer slope. Slate seemed to be in some pain, but he was moving all right, and cursing a blue streak. From the sound of his voice, he was going to survive.

"He's hit, but it's just a flesh wound, looks like," said Ben.

"Better be. That stupid bastard. He made an awful racket, poking his way down that slope. He near got his fool head blowed off for his trouble."

As Shorty and Slate reached the canyon floor, the two men left the unconscious Slocum lying facedown on the ground and walked over to meet them.

"I'm hurt," Slate acknowledged grimly.

Mat saw the stain on Slate's shoulder and ripped back the shirt. Leaning his face close, he inspected the hole left by the bullet. It was neat enough and high on Slate's shoulder. Not too much blood was oozing from the wound. "Can you move your shoulder?" he asked.

"Sure. There weren't no bones hit. It hurts to beat hell, but I think the slug went right on through."

"That's what I think, too."

"We'll get that girl to take care of you," said Shorty.

Ben smiled weakly. "Not likely," he murmured.

"Come on," Mat said, "we got ourselves a helper. We'll beat him a bit until he's good and tender, just to show him who's boss. After that he'll be happy to dig for us."

Shorty looked over at the unconscious figure. "He sure looks big enough."

"We'll cut him down to size. Don't you worry," Mat said.

They heard distant screams and halted in their tracks, listening. The sound seemed to come from the air directly over their heads.

"Jesus," said Ben softly. "What's that?"

"You think maybe it's Apaches?" Shorty wondered softly. "Maybe they caught someone?"

"Hell, I ain't seen an Apache since we left Mesa."

Mat cleared his throat and, shading his eyes, looked carefully around at the canyon rims. "You never do see an Apache," he told Ben. "Not until it's too late."

That quieted the four of them. They waited a moment longer. But there were no more screams, and they headed for the big sprawled figure of the man who was going to haul their gold out for them.

Slocum stirred painfully the next morning as Shorty aroused him from a fitful sleep, poking him in the ribs with a gun barrel. It wasn't just the shattering pain deep in his skull that made him grind his teeth, it was the aching ribs and what could have been a fractured arm. The four of them had whiskeyed themselves into a lather the night before and worked Slocum over pretty thoroughly. They were experts who enjoyed their work, and their announced intention had been to cut him down to size.

As Slocum pushed himself erect and blinked into Shorty's round, sun-baked face, he was willing to agree that they had succeeded in doing just that—for now.

"You ready to go to work?" Shorty asked, a grin on his face.

Grunting unintelligibly, Slocum sat up and looked around him. He was just inside the entrance of the mine these men were apparently working. Beside him, his thin back to Slocum, an old-timer was asleep, snoring softly and unevenly. The girl, bound and trussed with cruel effectiveness, was already awake. Sitting up with her back to a boulder, she was watching him alertly. He had heard them call her Topaz the night before.

When her eyes met Slocum's, she smiled fleetingly. He nodded agreeably and smiled back.

"Oh, you like Topaz, do you?" Shorty asked, smirking.

"Yes, you fat little son of a bitch, I do."

Slocum's insolence surprised Shorty. He thought they had succeeded in thoroughly cowing Slocum the night before. Shorty looked around at the others for some indication of how he should respond. The gray, balding fellow Slocum had wounded came over, his arm in a sling. His name was Slate. He glared unhappily down at Slocum and with careful deliberation kicked Slocum in the crotch. Because of his wound, Slate was a little off balance and his aim was not perfect, but he did enough damage to make Slocum bend over swiftly and bite his lip as the sudden excruciating pain stabbed through his groin.

"Bastard," Topaz said.

"Leave him be for now, Slate," the fellow with half a face spoke up. "If he's gonna help us, he's got to be able to stand up and walk. Ain't that right?"

"Sure, Mat," Slate said grudgingly, stepping back. "Just wanted to put him in his place, is all."

"He knows it. After last night he does, anyway."

Shorty woke up the old prospector then, poking him with the same enthusiasm he had shown on Slocum. The old man groaned pitiably, but managed to sit up without any help.

"Take the three of them into that new branch Blucher and I discovered yesterday, Shorty," Mat said. "Set them to work. I'll send Slate in to spell you in a little while."

"I ain't had breakfast yet."

Mat rummaged in a saddlebag and tossed some jerky at Shorty. "Chew on that," he told him. "And take in some water for yourself."

Shorty caught the jerky, took a bite and began to chew. "What about them?"

"Keep them digging."

With a shrug, Shorty untied the girl's wrists and ankles, then stood back and waited for her to get up. She found it difficult. Slocum saw her wince in pain as the blood flowed back into her hands and feet. She tried to stand but could not quite manage it. He could imagine the shock in her extremities as the blood rushed suddenly into them, the pain and the maddening pins-and-needles feeling. But she was game and in less than a minute or two she was on her feet, ready to move into the mine shaft.

Slocum got to his feet and helped the prospector to pull himself upright. The old man grumbled unhappily as he stared ahead of him at the mine shaft. Then he pulled free of Slocum and started in ahead of him. Topaz waited until he had passed her, then followed him in. Slocum entered last, Shorty on his heels.

Blucher lit three lanterns and handed two of them back. Topaz took one and handed the other to Slocum. After that Slocum and Blucher grabbed mud-coated picks and proceeded into the shaft. Slocum did not like what he saw. The timbers shoring up the walls and roof were rotting. In some places, less than half of a beam was still upright. Moisture was seeping through the walls in an almost steady stream, and before they had gone very far, the four of them were wading through ankle-deep water.

After what seemed to Slocum a considerable distance, they came to a fork in the shaft. One shaft led deeper, the other higher. The entrance to this second shaft appeared to have been cut out of the wall, and even by the dim light shed by their lanterns, Slocum could see at once that this new mine shaft had at one time been deliberately sealed off. It did not look very promising to him.

They moved on into it and kept going until they came at last to a solid wall of rock and pulled up.

Topaz held two of the lanterns to give Shorty light as he put down his lantern and lit some candles. With only this dim, flickering light to see by, the two men—under Shorty's close scrutiny—approached the wall and began flailing away at it with their picks. For at least an hour they labored without pause and without any appreciable result. Once before Slocum had been forced to mine, and he now realized that there was no way they were going to get gold or anything else from this solid rock face unless they used dynamite.

Mopping his brow with the back of his wrist, Slocum held up and stepped back to view the damage he and Blucher had done. As he had thought, it was negligible.

"We need some dynamite," he told Blucher. "We're getting nowhere this way."

"I know," said Blucher, "but this does not matter. Keep working. I will tell you why later."

"Tell me now, damn it!"

"What are you two mumbling about?" Shorty demanded.

Slocum spun to face Shorty. "We need some dynamite."

"Well, you ain't gettin' any. You got a strong back. Use it!"

As Shorty spoke he moved closer, a grin on his round, oafish face. Though he was still covering them with his Colt, the muzzle was no longer pointing alertly up at them. It was an older Colt, Slocum had noticed at once, with a barrel seven and a half inches long, making the weapon as heavy as a sinful heart. It had been in Shorty's hand since he entered the mine and more than likely he was just a little weary of holding it constantly on them.

Slocum's own cross-draw rig was empty, of course. After slugging him, they had taken his .44. He did not know if they had searched through his bedroll yet and found the old .36 Navy Colt he carried there just in case. He hoped not.

Turning to face Shorty, Slocum smiled. "If you want us to bring out any gold from this place, you'll just have to get some dynamite."

Shorty pulled up quickly. John Slocum was a tall man, better than six feet. In the narrow passageway, he loomed over Shorty. Despite the sudden flashing smile on his swarthy face and the friendly gleam in his green eyes, there was something distinctly ominous in his manner.

Shorty took a small, nervous step backward. "Well, damn it," he said unhappily, "I can't *get* you no dynamite. We don't have none. This here crazy prospector said all we had to do was pick up the nuggets. He didn't say nothing about dynamite."

Slocum turned casually to face the old man. "That right, Blucher?"

Blucher cleared his throat to speak. Out of the corner of his eyes, Slocum saw Shorty lean around Slocum as he waited expectantly—hopefully, even—for Blucher to confirm what he had just said. With the speed of a striking rattler, Slocum reached out and grabbed Shorty's gun hand about the wrist. Using both hands, he twisted violently outward. There was a sickening crack as the bone in Shorty's wrist gave way. With a muffled scream, Shorty dropped his weapon and sank to his knees, his left hand grasping his broken wrist. He began to blubber. In a moment, Slocum knew, he would begin to scream for help.

Snatching up Shorty's Colt, Slocum clubbed him on the head. Without a sound, Shorty collapsed forward onto the damp ground.

Topaz, still holding the two lanterns, smiled at Slocum. "You have the raven hair of an Indian," she told him, "and you strike like the Apache."

"Afraid not, ma'am. Name's John Slocum. I hail from Georgia."

"I do not understand about this Georgia. All I know is what my eyes and ears tell me. And my heart. I like you, John Slocum."

"The feeling is mutual, Topaz. But for now, at least, we've got other matters to consider." Slocum turned to Blucher. "You want to explain what's going on here? Where's all the gold this Shorty was expecting? And those other three outside? And why did you want us to just stand there and poke at that rock face for the rest of our lives?"

"There is no gold here," Blucher told him grimly. "Topaz and I know this. We saw these men on our trail and led them to this here abandoned mine I knew about. I just wanted to discourage them."

"It don't look like they discourage easy."

The old man scratched his grizzled face and nodded quickly. "That's a fact, mister. That's a fact. Anyways, there is such a mine as Shorty spoke of. It's the Dutchman's, and I have a map he gave me."

"The Dutchman?"

"Sure! The Dutchman, Jaccb Waltz. Ain't you never heard of him and his mine? Well, he gave me the map before he died. Yes sir, he did. And this here map he gave me shows the location of the mine he discovered years ago."

"This map—do you still have it?"

Blucher tapped his buckskin shirt and grinned like a baby. He had no teeth. "It's right here. Topaz done sewed it into the lining. It makes the shirt hot, but the heat warms my old heart. Those four have searched me over and over, but they ain't never thought to look where Topaz sewed it."

"All right, then. The next step is to get out of here."

The old man's grin vanished. "How we goin' to do that?"

"There's three of them still out there," Topaz warned him.

"I have Shorty's gun. It may be all we need. Give me one of those lanterns, Topaz."

Turning suddenly, Slocum beckoned to Topaz and Blucher to hold up. The old man stopped and crouched down, Topaz doing the same. Slocum had already told them not to emerge from the mine until he called to them. Turning back around, Slocum continued toward the mine entrance. It had been a bright pinpoint of light when first he saw it. Now the rectangular entrance dazzled him. Moving slowly and carefully so as to give his eyes a chance to adjust once more to the brilliant Arizona sunlight, he finally reached the entrance and flattened himself behind one of the timbers.

He listened carefully. Mat Wall was talking quietly to Ben Stringfellow. The two were discussing the situation. They were not arguing, but there was a querulousness in Ben's voice that told Slocum he was getting impatient with the way things were going— or not going.

Slocum stepped boldly out into the bright day, the big Colt in his hand waist high and level.

To the left of him, Slate Cadey was slumped crookedly forward, his back to the canyon wall, asleep. He had no weapon that Slocum could see. Ben Stringfellow, his back to Slocum, was hunkered just beyond Slate, poking idly at the ground with a crooked branch. Mat Wall was standing on the other side of Slate, staring directly at Slocum.

Wall was so astonished at Slocum's unexpected appearance that instead of immediately reaching for his sidearm, he froze. Slocum smiled and raised the

Colt. Only then, too late, did Wall claw for his sidearm. Slocum fired low, catching Wall in the flesh of
his right leg. The round slammed his leg out from
under him. Spinning, his arms flailing wildly, he went
down hard, striking the back of his head. He groaned,
tried to sit up, then collapsed back down, unconscious.

Stringfellow was on his feet by this time, his gun
half out of its holster.

"Freeze!" said Slocum, lifting his gun calmly and
sighting down the long barrel at Stringfellow's midsection.

Stringfellow froze.

"Now drop it," Slocum ordered.

The gun clattered to the ground.

Fully awake by this time, Slate swore angrily, but
made no attempt to go for a weapon. His arm was
still in a sling. He looked bad.

"Drop your gunbelt, too, Ben," Slocum told him.
"And where's my sidearm?"

"Over there."

With a flick of his head, Ben indicated Slocum's
bedroll lying with some saddles and other gear piled
alongside the canyon wall. Ben's gunbelt slipped to
the ground.

"Now back up!"

As Ben took a step back, Slocum called out to
Blucher and Topaz. Then he went over to his gear
and rummaged a moment until he found his own
.44 and his Winchester. A moment later, breath-
less, Blucher and Topaz emerged from the mine
entrance.

Slocum directed Blucher to pick up Slate's gunbelt
and sidearm. The old man wasted no time. As he

dropped Ben's six-gun into the holster, his eyes gleamed with a lively malice as he surveyed his three tormentors. The sight of Mat Wall lying flat on his back, as cold and as motionless as a dead rattler, seemed to give him a special pleasure.

"What're we going to do with them?" he asked Slocum.

"Got any ideas?"

"String 'em up by their balls!" the old man declared.

Topaz smiled brilliantly at Slocum. "Give them to the Apache woman," she said.

Slocum sighed wearily. "I was thinking of herding them into the mine. It's nice and cool in there. We could truss them good and proper, then roll a stone over the entrance. It would give them a chance, anyway. If they could get free of their bonds, they might be able to get out in time."

"You are too soft!" snapped Topaz. "We should kill them and be done with it."

"No."

Topaz shook her head in disappointment. "Maybe you are right. There is no Indian blood in you. No Apache."

Slocum flashed a grin at her. "Like I told you, I'm just a little ol' Georgia boy."

"Well, let's get to it then," said Blucher. He looked at Stringfellow and Slate. "All right, you two—grab that one-eyed son of a bitch and carry him into the mine. Move!"

"I can't," whined Slate Cadey. "I'm hurt. Hurt bad. This here wound in my shoulder ain't gettin' any better."

"Well, now, ain't that too bad!" said Blucher, striding over to Slate.

It looked as if the old man were about to pull his foot back and kick Slate up onto his feet. But before he could do anything of the sort, Slate grabbed a Colt he had hidden in his sling and fired up at Blucher. The round caught the old man high in the chest and flung him back against Stringfellow.

As both men collapsed to the ground, Slocum put his shoulder down and rushed Slate. Catching Slate in the midsection he drove him back, then down, his full weight on him. Crying out in genuine pain, Slate writhed in agony beneath Slocum, entirely forgetting his weapon. Slocum wrested it from him, then stood up.

"John Slocum!" Topaz cried. "Watch out!"

He swung around and saw Stringfellow trying to wrest his gun back from the wounded Blucher.

The moment he saw Slocum turn his way, Stringfellow sprang back from Blucher, holding both hands up and away from his body.

"All right, Slocum!" he cried. "All right. No need to shoot!"

Slocum looked back down at Slate. Eyes closed, moaning softly, Slate still lay on his back, his hand closed tightly about his shoulder wound. Blood was seeping through his fingers—black blood.

"Topaz, see to Blucher," Slocum said. Then he turned to Stringfellow. "Drag Wall into the mine. Slate, get up and follow him in."

Stringfellow grabbed Wall by his shirt collar and dragged him just inside the mine entrance, out of the sun. Slate was able to get onto his feet and drag himself in after Stringfellow. As soon as he was inside, however, he sank down, still clutching at his shoulder, moaning slightly. Mat Wall was still unconscious.

Topaz hurried in to Slocum. "The old man is hurt bad," she told him.

"You think you can tie these gents up the way they tied you up?"

Topaz nodded swiftly, eagerly. She hurried back out and returned a moment later with some rawhide. As she tied Stringfellow's hands behind him, Slocum kept his .44 trained on the man. Topaz was enjoying her work. When Stringfellow winced at the way the rawhide cut into his ankle, she smiled wickedly and tightened it still more. Slocum left her the gun he had taken from Shorty and told her to tie up Shorty when she finished with Slate and Wall. Then he went outside to see to Blucher.

Topaz had not exaggerated. Amos Blucher was severely wounded. The slug had caught him in the chest just above the lungs, shattering his collarbone. Where it had ranged from there, Slocum could not tell, but it had not come out. The bullet now rested somewhere deep in the old man's chest, more than likely in his right lung.

There was no time now for rolling any stones against the mine entrance or shoring it up in any way. They had to saddle up and move out fast, back to Mesa, where Amos Blucher could find a doctor to take out that bullet. Otherwise, he was never going to get to spend all that gold waiting for him in the Dutchman's mine.

• • •

Earlier that same morning, Tate Rawson awoke to find he was still alive, that during the night he had not been devoured by wild animals, attacked by Apaches, or stung to death by scorpions or rattlers. In this hideous, sun-blasted crater of the moon, there was still some mercy after all.

He had come to rest after the first exhausting flash of panic in a small, damp cave. There he had remained for the rest of the day, lapping like a beast at the water which streamed, icy and sweet, through the cracks in the striated wall of rock out of which his shelter had been scoured. He knew that he must be careful. If there should be a cloudburst in the mountains to the west, the sudden flood waters would leap and roar down through this canyon as if through a storm drain, sweeping into his cave and out again, smashing him to a pulp in the process.

But he was too exhausted to care. And there had been no rain for weeks in this parched region.

The night was so chilly that he woke up before dawn, shivering violently. But he got up, refreshed by what sleep he had been able to manage and the water he had been able to lap into his mouth. He was saner now that the heat was no longer such a terrifying threat. With incredible patience he managed to fill his canteen from the tiny, trickling streams of water that oozed out of the rock wall. This accomplished, he returned to the cleft where he had waited for Slocum. Slinging his bags over his shoulder, he stuck his revolver into his belt and headed in the direction of the shots he had heard the day before.

It was still cool. The sun had not yet managed to climb above the canyon's walls, so he stayed close to the walls and made good time. Coming upon a cleft in the rock face that seemed to lead in the direction from which those shots had come, he entered it, found himself in a narrow draw, and followed it into another canyon. This one was much larger and a clear stream meandered through it.

He had been out of water for some time. Splashing heedlessly into the shallow stream, he filled his canteen, drank greedily, then filled it again. The sun was pouring down from directly overhead. Glancing up, he saw its light filling the sky, radiating out in all directions like an explosion. He looked quickly away and hurried back to the canyon wall, grateful for whatever shade he could find, and kept going.

Almost at once Rawson heard what sounded like the muffled cries of wild animals emanating from deep within a cave. He pulled up to listen. The crying or calling or whatever it was came and went. He started up again and was soon able to make out one voice periodically calling out for help. There was a note of defiance in the call, but Tate sensed the desperation as well. When he got close enough, he thought he heard men arguing.

Moving around a shoulder of rock, he saw a grassy sward hidden away in a small, shaded draw—and horses grazing, four of them. Beyond the horses he saw the entrance to a mine and in front of the mine a campfire which had long since burned itself out. Around the dead campfire he saw a clutter of gear, a coffeepot, saddles, bedrolls, and slickers.

His heart had leaped when he saw the horses. The sight of all that gear pleased him almost as much. He picked his way through the clutter of gear and stepped cautiously into the mine shaft.

"Who's that?" he heard from the smothering blackness at his feet.

"Never mind who I am," Tate replied. "What's going on here?"

"Damn it! Get over here and loosen this rawhide. My wrists are nearly sawed in two."

By this time Rawson's eyes had adjusted to the dimness. Streaming in behind him was enough light for him to see clearly the man he was addressing. The fellow was sitting with his back to the wall, his hands tied securely behind him, his ankles bound also.

At first Rawson thought the dim light was playing tricks on him. But he soon realized that the man's face was actually as fearsome as it at first appeared. His cheekbone was caved in and there was an awful hole where his eye should have been. What looked like an eye patch had slipped up onto his forehead.

Alongside this one-eyed gent another man was lying on his side, staring wide-eyed at him. He was shivering violently and his lips were drawn back from his broken, ragged teeth in a kind of fierce grin. It reminded Rawson of a dog he had beaten to death once. When the dog finally sagged to the ground, its mouth was still frozen into that tight, grinning snarl.

Another fellow, very lean, was watching Rawson closely. His back was to the wall also and he had drawn his spare, stick-like knees up close to his face.

It was this one who spoke up next. "Hi, there, mister. Where in hell did you drop from?"

Rawson smiled thinly. "Just moseying through. You want to tell me what happened here?"

"Untie us first," the one-eyed one barked.

Rawson walked over to him and looked behind him. There was just enough light for him to be able to see how tightly the rawhide had been wound around the man's wrists, then bound in turn to the timber behind him. His ankles were bound up just as tightly. He glanced at the man shivering rigidly on the floor. He too was bound securely. The other fellow sitting with his knees up to his face was just as helpless.

Rawson looked down at One-eye. "You ain't in no position to bargain, the way I see it. So tell me what this is all about."

The fellow with the one eye looked up at Rawson for a moment, as if considering whether or not he deserved a reply, then glanced over at the long-legged fellow beside him.

"How you doin', Ben?" he asked the man.

Ben shrugged, then smiled up at Rawson. "Look, friend," Ben said reasonably, "you help us, we'll help you—and point you to a very pretty half-breed and a mountain full of gold. You savvy?"

Rawson did not need these men. All he really needed was waiting for him now outside this mine entrance. He would find food in those saddlebags, he knew, and there had to be extra canteens and weapons. He sure as hell could use the extra firepower. And there were four horses. He could take two of them to use in relay. In a couple of days he would be out of this hellish place and on his way north to Canada, where John Slocum would never find him, never in a million years.

But still, who were these men? And what did they mean by a mountain full of gold? And then—what he really needed to know—did John Slocum have anything to do with this?

"I'm listening," Rawson said. "Tell me about the gold."

"And the breed?"

"Yes, the breed." Rawson smiled bleakly. "It's been a long time for me."

They told him. At mention of the Dutchman's mine, his interest picked up, especially when John Slocum entered the picture. When they had finished, Rawson had the entire picture—all he needed to know.

Yes, he'd go to Canada, he decided. But first he'd see about that mine and that breed, and maybe take care of John Slocum while he was about it.

He started from the mine.

"Hey!"

Rawson stopped and looked back. It was One-eye who had called to him. "I'm leavin', gents," Rawson told him coldly. "I got other business."

"You leave us here like this and we'll come after you. That's a promise. We'll find you and kill you— slow."

"You'll have to get free first," Rawson taunted.

"We will."

Rawson smiled. "Well, you won't get far without horses."

"Damn you! Damn your miserable hide! I'll find you if I have to ride through the gates of hell to do it!" One-eye declared.

"Yup," Rawson told him, turning his back on him and stepping out into the sunshine. "That's just what you'll have to do."

3

In order to get out of the canyon the day before, Slocum had taken the same narrow game trail he had used to get into it. The trail was as steep and as treacherous as he had remembered it. Blucher had a difficult time staying on his horse. Topaz was a superb rider, however. She kept her pony beside the old man's, helping him to cling to his saddle horn. At last they reached the rim and started for Mesa.

The afternoon sun was pitiless, and it soon became obvious to Slocum and Topaz that Blucher could not make it. His saddle by this time was slick with blood, and though his old hands clasped the horn with desperate strength, his eyes were closed and his head lolled as loosely as a rag doll's. When his black hat finally toppled from his head, Slocum pulled up and dismounted.

"Help me get him down," he told Topaz.

She slid from her saddle and hurried to his side. Together, they pulled the old man off the slick saddle and carried him over to a clump of scrub pine. As soon as he was on the ground, Blucher opened his eyes.

"Water," he murmured, his voice a dry rattle.

Slocum unscrewed his canteen and started to hold it up to Blucher's mouth, but Topaz took it from him, then slipped her arm under Blucher's head and lifted him so he could drink it. Some color returned to Blucher's parchment-like face and he managed a smile.

"Just leave me here, Topaz," he told the girl. "This place is as good as any other."

"We are taking you to Mesa," she protested, "to a doctor."

"No, you ain't. I'm a dead man, sure as you got Apache blood."

"No need to talk like that," Slocum said.

"Don't argue with me!" the old man cried, his rheumy eyes blazing with sudden fire. "I don't want to go no farther! I want to rest. I'm tired." Then he leaned his head back and smiled up at Topaz. It was a weak, brave smile. "I'm dead tired, Topaz. So please just let me be."

Topaz looked at Slocum and nodded sadly.

Slocum screwed the cap back onto his canteen and

stood up. Realizing the two wanted to be left alone, he walked over to his horse and looped the canteen over the saddle horn.

When he looked back at them, they were talking quietly. Once or twice he thought he heard Topaz laugh. The old man lifted his hand once and held his palm against the girl's cheek. She took his old hand in hers and kissed it. A moment later he thought he heard her cry out. Then she bent to kiss his thin, bronzed forehead, after which she bowed her head abjectly for a moment, hugging herself and rocking slightly.

As he started toward her, she stood up and walked toward him. There were no tears marring her olive face, but her large, almond-shaped eyes were filled with sorrow.

"He is dead," she told Slocum. "When we bury him, I will take his shirt."

Slocum nodded. "And the map."

"Yes, the map, too. He wanted me to have it."

"We don't have any tools to dig a grave with, but I don't like leaving him here for the buzzards."

"Leave it to me, white man. I will find a place. No wild animals shall feast on his flesh. I promised him that."

"My name is John. Call me John."

She seemed about to make a sharp retort, but evidently thought better of it. With a sigh, she smiled wanly. "All right. I will call you John. Stay by the old man. I will return soon."

She mounted up and rode off. Slocum busied himself watering his horse, then unsaddling it and rubbing it down thoroughly while he waited for her. She was gone a long time. It did not worry him. He knew she would return. The old prospector sleeping that long, long sleep in the scrub pine behind him was assurance of that.

The baleful red eye of the sun was sitting on the horizon when Topaz returned. She dismounted and walked toward him, leading her pony.

"I have found a place," she told him.

Slocum nodded and together they walked over to the dead man. Topaz took Blucher's shirt off, folded it neatly, then placed it in her bedroll. Working together, they wrapped Blucher in his slicker and tied him securely over his saddle. With Topaz in the lead, Slocum led Blucher's horse. They traveled for close to an hour, heading almost directly west, until they reached another plateau, beyond which they picked their way carefully down into a narrow canyon. It was another hour before Topaz pulled up finally and dismounted. It was almost completely dark by this time.

Slocum dismounted also.

"There," she said. "In that cleft."

Topaz was pointing to a ledge at least six feet high and about ten yards off the trail.

"We aren't going to cover him?"

"From there the vultures cannot see him, and the wolves and coyotes cannot reach him. There are stones nearby. We can wedge them in close beside him so that no one will know he sleeps there."

Slocum nodded.

"Let's get it done," he said.

Two hours later and about five miles farther down the canyon, they built a campfire. As it blazed in the darkness, sending light dancing against the sheer walls enclosing them, Topaz sat cross-legged before the fire, studying the Dutchman's map intently.

Lighting a quirly, Slocum sat down across from her and watched. In the leaping firelight, her features were even more impressive. Her long dark hair sometimes took on red highlights. Her luminous eyes appeared fathomless. She had been wearing a loosefitting skirt and blouse typical of the Spanish women of the area, but ill usage had torn one shoulder to tatters, so that a flap of it hung down now off her bronzed shoulder. She appeared totally unaware of what effect this had on Slocum. At last she folded the map carefully and slipped into her bedroll. Then she glanced across the fire at Slocum. She contemplated him for a long while without speaking.

He was about to say something when she stood up, turned, and moved away into the night. After a while he heard her returning, striding through the darkness beyond the fire. She materialized out of the blackness like an apparition, caught suddenly in the firelight— stark naked. Without pause, she walked around the fire and came to a stop inches from his upraised face.

He flicked his quirly away and came to attention, but warily.

"I have just tasted death," Topaz told him, her Spanish accent more pronounced than before. "Now I want life. Do you understand, John Slocum?"

"That's not so hard to understand," he told her. "I been thinking along them lines myself."

"Good. I have made a soft bed for us of pine boughs and pine needles."

She reached down and took his hand. He rose and

followed her into the darkness.

The bed she had made was in the cup of a rocky formation. Her slicker and a blanket had been placed down upon the pine boughs. Overhead the moon watched, brighter than a silver dollar. She threw herself lightly down upon the blanket and turned to face him. The moonlight cast a sheen over her body. She scissored her thighs slightly apart, and he became suddenly aware of her fingers moving in that dark patch of curls between her legs.

The sight of it hit him like whiskey on an empty stomach. His mouth dry, the hot blood beating in his brain, he shucked off his clothes and lay down on the blanket beside her. He ran a hand down her belly to trap those fingers tucked between her thighs.

"You sure you are not Indian?" Topaz asked.

"Not right this here minute, I ain't."

"You want me?"

"Like you said, I'm sick of death."

She looked down at him and smiled. "Good. You are ready."

He moved against her and felt the hard tip of himself probe up into the warm moist cup between her thighs. She raised one thigh to give him entrance, and he plunged slowly into her and stayed there. Her breathing came faster, shallower. He smiled and withdrew slowly, then plunged in again. This time she made a little sound and eased herself around until her breasts and face were flat against the blanket. She was like a large, silvery cat in the moonlight, crouched to spring.

He pulled out all the way, swiftly, seized her hips and dragged her up onto her knees. Kneeling between her widespread thighs, gripping her just where her hips curved up to meet her belly, he rammed deep into her, all the way to the hilt. She grunted and drove back against him like a coiled spring.

"Good!" she muttered. "Yes, yes!"

He reared upright, gripping her with both hands, driving into her, out and in, watching her little fingers clutching at the blanket, her head turned to one side so he could see her mouth open and slack, her face pressing against the blanket with every heaving lunge.

He slowed then, teasing her, moving back when she moved back, forward when she moved forward, denying her what she wanted. She began to snarl at him. Her hand reached back to grab him, claw him, if possible. Unable to reach him, she began to whimper as she tried to recapture the rhythm. She rose up onto her elbows, crouched there, then came all the way back, crying out, "Now! Now! Damn you, White Eyes!"

He laughed and rammed full force to meet her backward lunge, his hands sinking into her flesh, his hips driving into her. He caught a glimpse of her breasts jiggling, saw her head come back, her face lifting up toward the sky, her mouth open, and he couldn't hold it back any more. He felt it surging up within him, driving him on and on until he had driven her right back down onto her face, and he came in her, lunging and lunging again, falling forward onto her back, rolling her onto her side, her rump cupped up against his groin, holding her to him with one strong arm across her breasts.

They lay that way for a long time, not talking, their breathing slowly subsiding.

"I think maybe it does not matter if you are Apache," she said softly at last. "You are mean like an Indian."

"You aroused me," he told her.

She rolled away slightly so that he could see her, all of her, bathed in the moonlight. It was as if she were inviting the moonlight to impale her. He ran a hand up her flank, soft and slow up the curve of her side, then down again, and slowly up again, and across the soft swell of her breasts, feeling her nipples drag along the roughness of his palm, and then back again, almost rough against her breasts' buoyant resilience, and then down again, slowly, all the way to her knee, and slowly up again.

She moaned softly and lifted her arms above her head as she opened herself to the stroke of his fingers as they moved up the inside of her thighs. She spread her legs luxuriantly. Her head went back and her eyes closed, while she soaked up the feel of what his hand was doing to her. Through his palm he could feel what his touch was making her body feel.

He glanced down at himself. He was ready again, straining to impale her. Swiftly, he eased himself up onto her, sinking deep inside her. What came then was totally different from the first time. It was as if the silver moonlight had fused them, turned them into one single, throbbing body, expressing an endless rhythm that brought them slowly close and slowly back and slowly close again, hips moving in long, sweet reaches. When at last the pace began to build, it wasn't he who made it build, nor she, but both of them fused together into one single rising tide of feeling.

Even when they exploded, there was no lunging

apart, no hard breathing, only a series of gasps as together they writhed and clung to each other until the storm had passed.

At last they pulled apart. He looked down at Topaz and saw her looking at him with eyes filled with wonder and something else he couldn't define. Was it fear, perhaps?

"Was that Indian enough for you?" he chided softly.

"There is tenderness in you, John."

"And in you as well."

"Yes. When the animal is fed, then there is tenderness. You are a big man, John. A very big man."

He smiled. "I know."

"That is not what I mean," she chided.

Swiftly, she reached up and pulled his head down upon her breasts. Stroking his hair, she began to hum softly. It was a Spanish tune Slocum had heard in a small *cantina* along the border years before. He closed his eyes and let her song lull him.

Then he thought of something. "That old man, Blucher. Did you love him?"

"Yes."

"The way you just loved me?"

"Yes. It took much work, but he was so sweet and so grateful when it happened, I loved to do it for him."

"I think that makes you a big girl, too," he said, kissing her.

She responded to his kiss and he felt himself begin to rise again, and she felt it, too, and looked at him, a sudden, impish smile on her face. She shifted her body down so that they fit together, all the breath going out of her as he sank deep into her again.

Afterward, they lay silent for a long while, Topaz on her back beside him. He was stroking her breasts, content not to talk, just to feel.

It was Topaz who spoke first. "I will not share the gold, John Slocum," she told him. "Not unless you swear allegiance to me."

"Swear allegiance? The last time I did that, the South went to war with the North, and I lost Slocum's Stand."

"I am serious."

"I am, too."

"This gold is not for me. Not all of it. Amos Blucher knew that, too. He was willing to help me, to share the gold with me."

"Now just what do you have in mind, Topaz?"

"I will not tell you. Not now. I ask only that you trust me."

"I came into this sun-blasted wilderness to look for a murderer. I didn't come looking for gold. You can trust me. The man I want is still at large."

"And I must find the mine. It is still well hidden."

Slocum shrugged. "That makes us even. I have my job to do, you have yours. It's all right, Topaz. For now I'll let you call the shots."

"That is not good enough, John Slocum. I must have your allegiance."

"Couldn't you tell a minute ago that you already had it?" he asked.

"Perhaps I could. But it is hard for me to trust a white eyes."

"Give me a chance, Topaz. I might surprise you."

She smiled then. "You have already surprised me."

"I think we better get back to the camp."

"No. It is safer here, away from the fire. I will keep you warm."

He saw the wisdom of that and let himself be enclosed in her arms. For a short while he was aware of her stroking his hair, then nothing as he sank into a delicious sleep.

When he awoke the next morning she was gone.

It was not at all difficult for Rawson to pick up the trail left by Slocum and the two others the day before. The climb out of the canyon offered some problems, but he gained the plateau above the canyon by mid-morning and set off after the still fresh tracks. He had decided against taking more than one horse. If he was going to track Slocum, he'd best travel light.

He had not gone far when he saw a girl crossing the trail half a mile or so ahead of him. One glimpse and he knew this was the half-breed who had gone off with Slocum and the old prospector. She was riding due west, heading deeper into the mountains. As he watched, she took a narrow trail that led into a canyon below.

But where were Slocum and the old man?

Rawson pulled his horse back off the trail so she would not see him, waited for her to pass, then took after her. She would know where Slocum was—and the map, too, maybe.

As soon as the girl had ridden out of sight, he nudged his mount toward the canyon. He did not intend to take the girl until she stopped at noon.

As soon as Rawson stepped out of the mine entrance, Ben Stringfellow bent his body forward until his face was inches from his ankles. With a dexterity born of desperation, he leaned just an inch closer and resumed gnawing on the last strand of rawhide still binding his ankles. He could only close his teeth over the rawhide once or twice before having to straighten himself up again. But he was patient. And in less than an hour he had freed his ankles.

"You're a bloody snake, that's what you are," said Mat.

"We ain't free yet," Ben replied.

"I know that, damn it!" Mat snapped.

It took a while for Stringfellow to be able to put much pressure on his feet, the ankles were so painful. But when he could, he used them to drive himself back against the timber to which his wrists had been tied. He was patient and each time he rammed himself back against the timber, it gave only a fraction. But it was rotten at its base already, and he knew it would have to give way eventually.

It came loose where he had thought it would, at the base. As he yanked forward with all the power in his shoulders, the timber slid out from the wall. At once, ignoring the thin tracery of silt and debris that immediately began to pour down from the rotten beam the timber had been bracing, he slipped his wrists over the end of it and then backed up to Mat Wall, raising his bound wrists as high as he could.

Wall's teeth were as sharp or sharper than Stringfellow's, and it wasn't long before Ben's wrists were free once more. He groaned slightly as the blood rushed back into his hands, but kept rubbing them briskly together anyway to get the circulation going again. As soon as he was able, he untied Wall.

While Wall rubbed his wrists and ankles, String-fellow examined Slate. As he had thought, the man was dead. That left only Shorty. Ben turned to Mat. "I better go after Shorty."

"Go ahead," Mat said. "But don't take too long."

"Why?"

"That timber you dragged out weakened the ceiling. I figure this place is about to collapse any minute now. Look at that pile that's gathered already."

Stringfellow turned about and was astonished at the amount that had already sifted down from the spot he had weakened.

"Jesus," he said, peering up at the ceiling.

Even as he watched, a ceiling beam groaned, then plunged down, one end of it slamming hard into the ground. It sounded like a cannon shot when it hit. A second later a huge spill of dirt and rock roared down upon it, burying the beam and filling up half the shaft. From all sides then came the squealing and cracking of timbers as first one and then another began to give.

Neither man waited another second. "Forget Shorty!" Wall cried. "Run for it!"

Limping painfully, Wall darted out of the mine shaft one step ahead of Stringfellow. They got as far as the dead campfire when a terrific roar came from deep within the shaft and a cloud of dust and debris whooshed out the entrance, causing both men to turn away. When they looked back at the mine entrance, they saw an almost solid wall of dirt and rock.

"Poor Shorty," said Ben.

"Don't waste any sympathy on that stupid son of a bitch," Mat said. "He was the one who let Blucher and the girl get away."

"What now?"

"We go after that bastard who refused to untie us. We'll never find that girl and the Dutchman's mine now. She and that crazy old man know these mountains better than the Apaches. But that other son of a bitch—him we can find."

Stringfellow nodded and headed for the horses.

Topaz was in the act of saddling her pony when she saw the fellow striding toward her from the cover of some nearby rocks, his revolver leveled at her head. She put her saddle back down on the ground and swore. One look at him and she knew what he was and what he wanted. Something had told her she was being followed, but she had ignored the warning. She had known it couldn't have been John Slocum—not this soon, anyway—so she had just assumed it was her imagination.

That had been a mistake. A bad mistake.

"Who are you?" she demanded.

"Name's Rawson. Tate Rawson," the man said, pulling up in front of her. As he looked her over, he made no effort to hide his intent.

"I do not know you. Put down that gun and ride out of here. I warn you."

"Oh, do you now?" The man smiled.

Topaz did not like the smile or the man. His face was unshaven, his eyes red-rimmed, his lips cracked and broken. His forehead was wide enough, but the rest of his face almost tapered to a point, so that his chin was narrow and weak, his teeth slightly protuberant and yellow, like fangs. He resembled an insect someone had stepped on without killing.

But she knew enough not to underestimate the man. This white eyes was dangerous.

"Is it me you want?" she asked coldly, masking her contempt.

"That, too. But I want something else first. From what I hear, you know where that Dutchman's mine is hid. You and Amos Blucher."

"Blucher is dead."

"And Slocum? John Slocum?" Rawson asked.

"He has gone his way."

"Well, now, ain't that pleasant to hear?"

"And I think you should do the same. I do not know where the mine is. When the old man died, he did not tell me."

"I think maybe he did. I think maybe he had a map hid somewhere. That's what those gents you left in the mine said."

"They knew nothing. They would say anything to gain your help. Did you free them?"

"Hell, no. After what they told me, I figured I didn't want to share you or the gold with anyone."

Topaz took a step back. As she did so, the heel of her foot caught on her saddle, and she stumbled to the ground. She caught herself with her hands, but that left her defenseless as Rawson, seizing the opportunity, moved swiftly to take her.

Holstering his six-gun, Rawson tried to pin both of her wrists, but soon found he was dealing with a powerful and desperate antagonist, as difficult to hold as a tomcat in a flour sack. And how the hell could he get his pants down while he was wrestling? Sitting up quickly, he lashed out with his fist, intending to catch Topaz on the point of the chin just hard enough to stun her. But Topaz ducked back and he missed. The force of his carry-through left him off balance. Topaz took this opportunity to pull free of him, jump up, and snatch the bedroll she had set down beside her saddle.

Jumping to his feet, Rawson took after her with giant, hungry strides. Topaz was reaching into the bedroll for a knife when he caught her from behind and spun her about. The bedroll spilled open, the knife clattering to the ground. When he saw the knife, he smiled grimly and kicked it away, pulled her brutally toward him, and clipped her on the chin with his clenched fist. Her head rocked around and she dropped the bedroll, but she did not go down.

He stepped back, suddenly puzzled. He didn't want to have to punch her into insensibility. What was the fun of taking a woman who wasn't feeling anything, not even hatred?

And then he saw the piece of old paper—a parchment, it looked like—blowing away from the open bedroll. At the same time he saw it, she did. With a cry, she broke away from him and snatched it up.

He let her run with it for a while, a triumphant smile on his face, then unholstered his six-gun and fired over her head at a boulder in front of her. The sound the bullet made as it ricocheted back caused her to pull up. She turned then to face him. He was not through with intimidation, however. Aiming at the ground between her moccasins, he fired a second time, the round exploding the rock between her feet as it ricocheted away. He saw her wince as tiny shards of rock bit into her ankles.

"Now come here and be nice," Rawson said.

He ignored her eyes as she walked toward him. No man should have to withstand that concentration of pure, undiluted hatred. Rawson knew it would shrivel even his soul.

When she was a few feet from him, he held out his hand. "Let me see that map. That's what it is, isn't it? A map?"

She handed it to him without a word. Swiftly, he unfolded it. Yes, god damn it! That's just what it was! That crazy Dutchman's map! He could see the Dutch words in the margins, the barely legible lines and scrawls. But as he peered at it eagerly, he realized the crazy son of a bitch had not put any north, south, east, or west markings on it. How the hell could you locate anything in these mountains with a map like this?

He looked up at the breed. He had the distinct feeling that she knew precisely what he was thinking. He smiled and handed the map back to her.

"That's all right," he said. "I won't take you. And you can have your map back."

She took the map, folded it quickly, then bent to place it once again in her bedroll. He watched her lightning hands gather up the blankets and the rest of her things, then tie the slicker shut. When she had finished, he walked closer and grinned down at her.

She stood up and looked at him. "You want me to take you to the mine."

"Yes."

"You can't read the map. You need me to read it."

"Yes."

"What makes you think I can read it?" she asked.

"I got a good feeling about that. You wouldn't be

so anxious to hold on to it if it meant nothing to you. Mount up. I'll follow you."

With a fatalistic shrug, she turned away from him, bent, and grabbed her saddle. He made no effort to help her as she lugged the saddle over to her mount and dropped it onto the saddle blanket she had already placed on the horse. When she had finished tightening the cinch, he walked over to where he had kicked her knife, picked it up, and examined it. It was big enough and sharp enough to stop a bull buffalo in its tracks. He was sure he could use it.

He stuck it into his belt, watched her mount up, and walked over to his own horse.

4

At first Slocum was furious. But when he calmed himself down and thought it over, he realized how little Topaz owed him. And then he found himself laughing aloud at the ease of her deception. Before long, he was remembering as well her supple, dusky body bathed in moonlight, the passion in her dark, almond-shaped eyes, and the clean emptiness he felt even now.

When he reached the spot where he had lit the

campfire, he found that she had taken with her all of his gear, including his bedroll. With mounting apprehension, he hurried to the small arroyo where they had hobbled their horses. She had taken his dun, as well.

He was about to howl in fury when he caught something on the rock wall before him. Looking closer, he saw that Topaz had used a soft-edged stone to scratch an arrow on the rock face. The arrow pointed back along the way they had come. At once, he saw what she had done—stampeded his horse back up the canyon, perhaps after securing his bedroll and the rest of his gear to it.

At least that was what he hoped.

Studying the ground carefully, he saw the prints of her horse and that of his own. He followed them for some distance, then saw where the ground was suddenly torn up, with his horse's long strides abruptly outdistancing hers. So far, then, he had guessed correctly. It was at this point that she had stampeded his horse, probably by slapping its rump with her quirt.

He sighed. Already it was mid-morning. By the time he recovered his mount, Topaz would be far ahead of him, securely out of his reach in these treacherous mountains, while he would be free once again to resume his search for Tate Rawson. Somehow, he could not help feeling a bit disappointed at that weary prospect.

He would like to meet Topaz again some day, under another shower of moonlight, perhaps.

His eye on the tracks of his spooked horse, Slocum started off down the canyon. He trotted at first, but as soon as the sun blanketed him he realized he was courting disaster if he kept up such a pace, and slowed down. Keeping to the shade of the overhanging rock whenever he could, he made good time. With only half the morning gone, he rounded a clump of rock and saw the dun less than fifty yards from him, cropping the grass on a small island in the middle of a seep.

He pulled up in surprise and gratitude. The horse should have gone much farther, but in this heat the water and grass had held him. Slocum saw his bedroll tied securely to the cantle. Topaz had even looped his canteen about the saddle horn, just as he had hoped.

He was smiling when he mounted. Perhaps he should return the favor. A woman like Topaz would be hard to find a second time, and he was not getting any younger.

Rawson camped early that night, stopping at the first water hole he came to. He was hoping for some fun; the gold could wait. But when he approached Topaz in the darkness, he caught the hard gleam of her eyes and pulled up, uncertain. He had her knife, but God only knew what else she might have on her. Not that there was really any place left for her to hide anything.

Still, he decided he would hold off for now. Maybe he could suggest something later, after he showed her he wasn't such a bad egg. Maybe he could convince her to pleasure him just a little. He would promise not to take more than a handful of gold nuggets if she'd be nice to him. Maybe she'd believe that. Maybe.

He cleared his throat. "Just thought I'd see if you was all right." He grinned lasciviously through the darkness at her. "I wouldn't want nothin' to happen to as pretty a woman as you."

"Get back to your sleeping bag, pig. While you sleep, I will not kill you, but that is only because I want others to have that pleasure."

Her words shook him, like a fist coming at him out of the darkness. Cold sweat materialized on his forehead. He took a step backward and peered quickly around him into the shadowy night. On a peak high above them a coyote began to yap at the moon. It was as if the coyote were laughing at him. Then he thought of the snakes, the lizards, the scorpions, the spiders scuttling about in the darkness, and he shuddered. Backing up quickly, he left her and crept in under his slicker, but not before examining it carefully in the firelight. Wide-eyed, his revolver in his hand, he leaned his head against his saddle and tried to sleep.

He was still trying the next morning when the sun broke with sudden brilliance over the mountain ridge.

Before they set out that morning, Rawson watched Topaz consult her map. She did it deliberately, in full view of him. Watching her do this made him uneasy. It was like she was putting on a show just for his benefit. He was already exhausted from his sleepless night and he almost took out his six-gun and shot the damn map out of her hands. He was beginning to realize that it was not he who had her, but she who had him. It galled him and made him want to strike out at her, but his thinking was too fuzzy to settle on how.

She mounted before him and seemed to wait impatiently for him to mount up as well. When he had stepped into his saddle, he caught the faint glimmer of a smile on her face an instant before she turned around and booted her pony toward the canyon looming ahead of them.

"How much farther?" he shouted at her.

"It will not be long now," she sang.

He shuddered. Maybe he had better turn off and leave her right now, he thought blearily.

But he didn't. Through the gathering heat of another day they rode on endlessly, through canyons, up steep grades, their horses clawing at the shale, across sun-flooded ridges, twisting and turning, moving ever deeper into this blasted wilderness of stone and sand and cacti. He hated this land. Everything in it had a rattle, a thorn, or a sting.

They were following a streambed. There was no trace of water in it, only gravel and sand and a few dark patches. Topaz had been drawing steadily ahead of him and he was thinking of calling out to her, but his mouth was dry, his tongue heavy. Perhaps if he fired at her she would hold up. But he did nothing. A fatalistic weariness had fallen over him.

Topaz led him up the side of a steep draw. The last few feet made for a hard scramble, and his horse almost lost him, but he topped the crest and rode for a short distance along the ridge. A valley opened before them, dotted with saguaro. Black, gleaming rock rimmed the valley like sentinels. Rawson felt a little better riding into the valley when he saw the grass and the line of cottonwood and willow. That meant water. He urged his horse to a canter in hopes of overtaking Topaz. It was not yet noon, but he was more than willing to camp here now that they had found water.

He did not notice the startled bird that flew up out

of the mesquite just ahead of him and was about to call out to Topaz to slow down when four mounted Apaches broke out of the willow and with wild, shrill yells booted their ponies toward him. A second before he wheeled his horse, he saw Topaz pulling up, a look of savage triumph on her face as the Apaches streamed past her in their single-minded pursuit of him.

His horse was soon galloping flat out, as if it too knew what hellish damage an Apache could do. Its mane was flying, its nose thrust into the wind. Rawson glanced back. The distance between himself and the Apaches was lengthening. But when he turned back around, he saw four more Indians coming off the ridge he had just left. He swung his horse broadside and headed up the side of a draw. He reached the crest with eight Apaches on his tail, and raced along it until he found his way blocked by a wall of sheer rock.

Desperate, all thought of surrender washed out of him by the sheer terror the Apache could arouse in a white man, he wheeled his horse and grabbed for his six-gun. But the Indians were on him like fierce hornets, and before he could get a single shot off he was flung from his horse. He landed on his back. Stunned, his senses reeling, he watched the savages grinning down at him, and waited.

He heard Apache talk. It sounded like an argument. Then rough hands grabbed him and slung him face-down over his saddle. In a moment rawhide had been looped around both wrists and both ankles and tied together under his horse. There was a shout of laughter and the rawhide was suddenly yanked tight. The sound of his wrist and ankle bones cracking apart was like dim pistol shots.

Rawson heard a scream explode from him as he spun into a nightmarish universe of pain. When the horse started moving, he lost consciousness.

Slocum had picked up Topaz's trail just before he made camp the previous night. That morning, he had come upon the spot where she had joined up with another rider, one who had come upon her while she had stopped to water her horse. All this had been easy enough for him to read in the undisturbed sand of this bleak, waterless world. What he could not read in it was the identity of the other rider.

Not until he overtook them by mid-morning was he able to get close enough to glimpse the face of the man who had joined up with Topaz. It was Tate Rawson. How this had come about, he had no idea. But it was a fact, and all Slocum could do was thank his lucky stars. He had gone after ten dollars and come up with twenty.

He was almost upon them, following less than half a mile back and keeping to a ridge above their trail, when he saw the two of them riding into a valley. Topaz was by this time a considerable distance ahead of Rawson.

What happened then caused Slocum to pull up and quickly dismount. He pulled his horse off the ridge and ducked down behind some scrub pine, watching in fascinated horror as the eight Apaches tore after Rawson. Shortly after they disappeared from his sight, Slocum heard Rawson's scream and knew they had captured him.

He had wanted only one thing when he set out after Tate Rawson, his lifeless body draped over a saddle as he brought him back to Yuma. But at that moment, Slocum felt sorry for the man.

Before Topaz reached the Apache rancheria, she could smell it. It was a smell that brought back memories both painful and happy.

Her mother, Rosaria, had been captured by the Apaches when she was twenty-two and about to be married to a Mexican landowner. Often at night she had held Topaz in her arms and crooned to her, telling stories of the land and people she had lost when a fierce Apache warrior swept her up in his saddle and rode north with her to this place. That warrior had been her father, Emiliano.

Topaz remembered her father with kindness. Though he had beaten Topaz's mother more than once, he had never once struck Topaz and he had always been a kind and gentle father to her. She had always been proud to walk behind his pony whenever he returned from a successful raid, brandishing his fresh scalps and leading his string of new ponies. Often she had taken part with the other women when the white eyes who fought the Apache had been brought to their camp to serve as their amusement.

But her mother had never joined with her at these times, and soon Topaz herself was able to admit that something within her rebelled when she took part in such grim amusements. And it was at such times that she realized she belonged to her mother as surely as she did to her father. Her soul was neither Apache nor Mexican—it was both. And from the moment this became clear to her, she began to consider more and more often the possibility of leaving The People and returning to the land of her mother.

The day came when Topaz's father failed to return from a raiding party. Soon after, her mother died. Topaz left The People then and journeyed to Mexico, or at least to the border of that land. What she found there, however, was only contempt. All those she met thought of her as less than human. She was a half-breed, part Apache. It was soon clear to her what they felt she was good for, and why. Since she was a savage, she must be treated as such. The men she found used her and discarded her as easily as the cigars they smoked. And it was not long before she came to believe what they said about her, and the savage part of her that remained Apache made many a man regret the day he treated her with contempt.

And then she had met old Amos Blucher. He took her in and asked of her only that she cook for him and keep his two-room shack clean. That she also tended to his needs as a man was something he appreciated and treasured. At last she no longer felt like an outcast, a savage, without feelings. The old man had made her think of herself as a woman. The old man needed her, and in his frail, bony arms she had felt peace at last.

But now he was gone, and she was back with The People.

As she rode closer to the rancheria, she looked around her, searching the faces that crowded toward her pony. With a pang, she realized how familiar everything was: the sounds, the smells, the sad squalor of the encampment, with its low wickiups of brush or hides thrown over sticks. She saw captured army blankets which had been used instead of hides to cover a few wickiups. Ponies grazed freely, and in among the wickiups naked brown children ran about, playing with their hoops or sticks, though now they were pulling to a halt, their shouts dying away as Topaz and the rest of the party rode in.

Everywhere she looked she saw the flat, impassive faces of The People, the wide cheekbones, the square jaws. The men seemed shorter than they were because of their wide shoulders and deep chests. All of them were sinewy, powerful creatures, dark-skinned, with long black hair hanging to their shoulders. A headband to hold their long hair in place, a breechclout, and their high-topped moccasins were all most of the men wore. For a moment she almost expected her father Emiliano to push through their ranks and open his arms to welcome her home.

The powerful young chief, Naratena, was waiting to greet her. They were no longer enemies, but when she was a girl and he was her age, he had been especially cruel to her, as had most of the Apache boys. Just as she was now to the Mexicans and to the Americans, she was then to the Apache children—a half-breed. They were always quick to taunt her, to make her realize that though they had pure Apache blood in their veins, the blood of the despised Mexican ran in hers. That Naratena had been the most inventive of her tormentors she could not forget, though now it served her purpose to pretend, like Naratena, that none of it had ever happened. Men forget their cruelties almost instantly, she had long since realized, while women could never forget a single cruel word or blow.

Naratena was obviously pleased to see her, and managed to rearrange his face in what approximated a smile as she halted her pony before him and slipped from her saddle. She wasted no time in greeting him, pointing instead to the unconscious man stretched over the saddle of his horse.

"Thank you for sending your braves to rid me of this filthy coyote," she told Naratena in the Apache tongue. "He wants the gold I have promised you and the clan. He thought I was taking him to it."

Naratena frowned. "The old white eyes is not with you. He is dead?"

"Yes. He was killed by others who want this gold as well."

"It is strange what the white eyes will do to gain this yellow metal. I cannot understand it. It is good only for beads and ornaments, not for arrow heads or for knives. It is too soft."

"If it has value for the white eyes, and if they will give us rifles and bullets in exchange for this yellow metal, what does it matter?"

Naratena grunted. He agreed with her, but could say nothing. It was, she realized, difficult for an Apache chief to take counsel from a woman.

"What will you do with this one?" she asked.

"We will give him to the women tonight. We have fresh mescal. The fires will leap high and the spirits of our great warriors and chiefs will walk among us."

"You mean you will get drunk."

He looked at her. Only his eyes smiled when he said, "And you will stay in my wickiup. I have sent my other wives from it."

"It is an honor," she said.

"Yes."

Naratena walked past her then and spoke to the

Apache men who had just succeeded in cutting Rawson loose. The white man was still unconscious, lying face up on the ground. At a word from Naratena, a brave stepped quickly forward and bent over Rawson. His knife flashed in the sun, and with the skill of a surgeon he peeled a long strip of skin back from Rawson's right shoulder all the way to his groin.

The searing pain of this awakened Rawson on the instant. Eyes wide, he began screaming. Disgust and contempt showed on each dark visage. This white eyes had no soul. Another brave stepped forward with his knife, but Rawson jumped up and tried to run away on his shattered ankles. He succeeded only in sprawling facedown in the dust, to the vast amusement of the braves gathering around.

The women had rushed over by this time and watched with gleaming eyes as the second brave peeled another strip of skin back, the bloody strip reaching this time from Rawson's shoulder to his left buttocks. Rawson's screams escalated.

Naratena turned to the women and spoke. The white eyes was theirs to finish. But Naratena would beat each one of them if he died before the moon rose that night. Thanking him profusely, one of the oldest Apache women, a thin, white-haired scarecrow, leaped forward and grabbed Rawson's broken left foot. Another took the right one, and between them—the pack of squaws following gleefully after—they dragged Rawson, still screaming and pleading for his life, across the compound toward a cooking fire behind the first row of wickiups.

Naratena turned and walked back to Topaz. "If you wish, you may join the women. That is a miserable wretch you have brought us. He has no soul. But he will sing loud and long."

"I hated him from the moment I first saw him. His smell was bad too, like most white eyes. But I will let the women have him."

"That is good. Come, we will eat now in my wickiup. I have fresh meat, and when I was told of your approach, I had it prepared."

She nodded obediently and followed Naratena into his wickiup.

Slocum held up and peered through a tangle of brush. The Apache rancheria was lit up like Denver City. There were fires everywhere and the level of savage merriment could only be explained by firewater—or, more likely, mescal. Every once in a while, cutting through the drums and the wild yapping of the men and the shrill laughter of the women, came a high, keening scream. It probably came from what was left of Tate Rawson.

It no longer sounded like Tate. His vocal cords had long since plugged into a deeper sensibility than Tate had known. He was now every white man who had ever had his tongue ripped out, his balls sliced open, or his eyes scoured with hot coals. He was a human soul in torment, and the artistry of the Apache was such that his soul would remain in torment for an incredibly long time before finally giving up the ghost.

The Apaches had an explanation for this. A man with a strong soul would suffer much but would not become like a hysterical woman. With great dignity, he would simply leave his body when the time came. But a man with no soul would have nothing but his body for the Apaches to torment, and under the Apaches' skillful ministrations this soulless husk could last almost indefinitely.

Slocum had seen the young chief with Topaz earlier. They had attended a few of the leaping campfires and had had a bowl of mescal together. And when, a few minutes ago, she had followed her lord and master into his wickiup, she had appeared to be a quite dutiful Apache squaw. This didn't go with what Slocum knew of her, but he figured she knew how to play whatever game she was playing.

Slocum did not have much time. The only reason he had been able to get this far was due to the celebration. He wanted Topaz and he wanted the gold. She knew the way to that mine, so that meant he had to have her with him if he was to find it. His reason for riding into the Superstition Mountains had been to find Tate Rawson. He had a driving need to punish the son of a bitch. But Topaz had managed to take care of that chore all by herself.

What he wanted now, he realized, was more of Topaz, and what all other men coveted—enough gold to sit back and relax, for a while anyway. Ever since leaving Georgia he had been a drifter, caught up in one fool scrape after another, and all he had to show for it were calluses on his rump and bow legs, and maybe a few happy memories, dealing mostly with señoritas and other lonely ladies.

He wasn't complaining. It was just that if the gold was out there, along with a woman like Topaz to lead him to it, he figured he just might as well take a shot at it.

He inched closer to the chief's wickiup. He thought

he could hear voices coming from inside it. Voices, or maybe howling. With all the dancing and drumming and ki-yiing coming from around the campfires, he could not be sure what he was hearing. He kept moving, pulling himself along with his elbows, his bowie knife held in his teeth. In addition to his .44, he had stuck his Navy Colt into his belt. And all six chambers in each gun were loaded.

Reaching the wickiup, Slocum started to peel the hide back cautiously when he heard Topaz cry out in sudden pain.

A moment before, Naratena had climbed back on top of Topaz for the third time that day, grunting like a pig. Lying wearily beneath him, watching his savage mask of a face, Topaz found herself thinking of John Slocum and wishing she had not decided to give herself to this Apache who used her with such chilling lack of affection. Powerful and handsome though he was, Naratena disgusted her as much as those men in the border towns, and all the many others. John Slocum had not disgusted her.

Naratena's rutting grew even more frantic. He flung his head back, shaking loose his tangled, greasy hair.

"Aiee!" he cried out in sudden release.

Still in the mescal-intensified frenzy of his coming, Naratena reached down and grabbed Topaz's hair. Slamming her head down over and over, he continued to pump into her. He was riding her now like his favorite pony, with Topaz's hair serving as a rein. A sharp pain and colored lights exploded deep within her skull. She reached up and tried to pull Naratena's hands from her hair. In Apache, he cried that she was his war pony and that he was once again charging the pony soldiers.

"Like hell!" she cried in pure Anglo-Saxon as she thrust violently upward, then managed to roll out from under him.

He reached over to grab her, but she pulled back. Furious, he snatched up his knife and slashed at her. The blade caught her just under her right breast, slicing a neat line all the way to her waist. She cried out in sudden pain and outrage, then pulled up her breast to examine her wound. At first she could see nothing but a faint line. Then the blood came.

That was when the side of the wickiup was thrust swiftly back. John Slocum, knife in hand, burst through the frame and vaulted into the wickiup. Leaping at Naratena, he missed. Naratena tripped him and he went down. Looming triumphantly over Slocum, Naratena let out a piercing war cry and raised his blade over his head.

Striking with the speed of a rattler, Slocum thrust upward with his own knife.

Naratena gasped, then gazed down in wide-eyed wonder at the hilt protruding from his stomach. Pitching forward onto the dirt floor, he twitched once or twice, then settled down onto the knife with heavy finality. Slocum rolled him over and pulled the blade from his gut. It made an ugly, sucking sound. Wiping the blade off on Naratena's dusky thigh, he stuck it back into his sheath and looked at Topaz, frowning suddenly.

"He's cut you, Topaz."

"It is nothing," she said weakly.

He reached out and took her arm to draw her closer. As he examined her wound, there was concern on his face, and she felt her heart swell within her. "You must leave here, John Slocum."

"Like hell. Not without you," he said.

"But you have killed a chief of the Moon Dog Lodge of the Mescalero Apache!"

"I didn't think he was riverboat gambler."

"Do not joke about it. To kill a chief is very bad," she said seriously.

"There must be other chiefs who can take his place."

"Yes," she replied, frowning thoughtfully. "Santoro. He would be much better, I think."

Slocum looked back out through the opening he had cut through the wickiup's side. "The party is still on. We better move out now, while we still can. Get your clothes on. And try to wind something around your waist to stop that bleeding."

"You think I will go with you?" she asked.

"I am hoping you will. But you can stay here if you want."

Without hesitation, she tore her black underskirt into strips, then wound them tightly around her waist. It succeeded in stanching the surprisingly heavy flow of blood. Shrugging into her skirt and blouse, she pulled on her moccasins, then pulled her saddle and harness out of the corner where she had stashed them and shoved them toward Slocum. He took both from her and pushed them ahead of him out through the opening. She reached under a blanket and withdrew her map. Tucking it into her bedroll, she followed Slocum out of the wickiup.

Not long after, as she stepped into her saddle and

followed Slocum into the night, she became suddenly dizzy. The moon rocked crazily about her, and for a moment she was afraid she would pitch headlong from her saddle, but she managed to right herself and keep going. Slocum was with her. And that seemed to make all the difference.

Watching from a ledge overlooking the Apache rancheria, Ben Stringfellow nudged Mat Wall.

"You see what I see?"

"I see them," Wall grunted. "That son of a bitch went right in there and took her out of that chief's wickiup. He's got sand, that one has."

"And so has the girl," Ben said.

"And she's got the map."

"Yes," Ben said with satisfaction.

"So all we got to do is lay back and let them lead us to the mine. This time, we stay well enough back so they don't catch wise."

"Suppose they don't go for the mine," Ben said.

"Then we go for them. We got a score to settle."

Wall watched the two ride out and saw which way they were heading. It wouldn't be difficult to find their trail, he reckoned.

The sudden, panting screams of Tate Rawson came to them. Both men turned to peer at the blackened figure hanging down from the sapling the Apache women had bent over the fire. Rawson's face must have been roasted to a cinder by now and he was probably as blind as a bat, but he could still scream.

"Got to hand it to them Apaches," Wall said, shaking his head in admiration. "They sure as hell know how to settle a score."

Ben Stringfellow shuddered. "Yeah. Let's get out of here before we get a personal demonstration."

Chuckling, Wall followed Ben off the ledge and into the black ravine where they had tethered their horses.

5

By morning, Slocum realized that Topaz was not going to lead him to any gold mine, at least not in her present condition. Topaz was losing too much blood. It showed in the frightening paleness of her face and in the difficulty she was experiencing keeping up with him.

As soon as Slocum noticed how persistently Topaz was falling behind, he pulled up and let her lead the way. At once he saw how difficult it was for her to remain upright in her saddle. Booting his dun alongside her mount, he told her they were going to camp as soon as they found water. Topaz protested, but not very convincingly.

Reining in at the first water hole they came to, Slocum dismounted first and helped Topaz down from her saddle, then sat her down on a rocky shelf alongside the water hole. The small rock basin was catching, then disgorging water coming from a small steady rivulet, clear and cold, that flowed out of a dozen cracks in the shelving rock to their right. He emptied out the stale water from his canteen, filled it with fresh, cold spring water, and handed the canteen to her. She drank it down greedily, thanking him with a grateful smile. Then he asked her to unwind her makeshift bandage so he could inspect her wound.

Hunkering down before her, he examined the wound critically and saw at once that it did not look good. The wound was at least ten inches long, tracing a line that started just under her left breast and continued past her right breast, ending just beyond her rib cage. The wound was deepest in her right side.

In order to get a clearer picture of the wound, he dipped his bandanna into the water hole and wiped off the dried blood as gently as possible. Though Topaz was no longer bleeding as profusely as before, from several points along the gash blood was oozing in a steady, relentless stream. Naratena's knife had slashed deeper than either she or Slocum had realized at the time, and the edges of the laceration no longer oozing blood were raw and in some cases already showing a deep, angry red. He could not touch any part of the ugly slash without causing Topaz to wince in pain. That she allowed herself to show any reaction at all was simply more proof, if any were needed, that the wound was serious and already beginning to fester.

He straightened and looked down at her. "You need help, a doctor's help, Topaz. And we're too far from Mesa or Yuma to go back that way. Do you have any ideas?"

"Blucher's place. It is just outside Coppertown."

Slocum nodded. "I know the place. South of here. About five or six miles."

She smiled wanly up at him. "You do not know where you are, John Slocum. These mountains have tricked you. Coppertown is west of here, and it is more than five miles."

"How far?"

"Eight, maybe ten."

"Do you think you can make it that far?"

"If I cannot, you will help me."

"Yes, I will. Is there a doctor in Coppertown?" he asked.

She nodded. "A man with death in his eyes. He has bad lungs. They call him Lucifer Garrett. He gambles and drinks much, but he is a good man with bullet wounds and is tender to the women when the midwives ask his help."

"I guess that's the best we can do, Topaz. Ordinarily, with a knife wound like that, I'd cauterize it to seal it, but it's too long a wound, and we can't seem to stop the bleeding." His concern was evident in his tone.

She felt this concern and was grateful. "Do not worry, John Slocum. You will bring me safely to Coppertown."

He was humbled by her confidence in him. The only problem was that he found it difficult to share.

He helped her wrap the bandage back around her wound, trying to keep it tighter this time in hopes of stemming the bleeding. Then he helped her back up onto her pony.

The brief rest and fresh water seemed to have helped her. She rode well until the heat of the day caused her to wilt rapidly. He turned off the trail they were following and headed for a distant line of cottonwoods. By midday they were resting gratefully beside a stream fed by the runoff from the Superstition Mountains behind them. Topaz rested with her back against a cottonwood, dozing fitfully, obviously grateful to be out of the unrelenting grip of the sun. She was pale again, her eyes vacant at times, but all in all, he felt, she was holding up remarkable well.

They stayed less than an hour in the shelter of the cottonwoods before moving out once more. Sunbleached bunch grass, saguaro plants, and a few squat cacti covered the upland over which they rode, while far ahead of them, Slocum could see the humped backs of the foothills and the mountains beyond them. In the dark paws of those crouching foothills, Slocum knew, lay Coppertown, a mining town that boasted few amenities but plenty of saloons for the miners. From what Slocum had heard of the place, there was law there, of a sort—but nothing an honest man could count on.

They had left the Superstition Mountains well behind and the wasteland over which they now rode was slashed occasionally by twisting canyons and arroyos. Out of the canyons titanic, grotesquely twisted rock shapes towered, some on the distant horizon, others looming astonishingly close. They resembled monstrous beasts congealed in stone during some awesome cataclysm far back in time. Some were a scalded red, others gleamed like great, washed chunks of coal in the sun.

Soon Slocum noticed that the sun was being obscured by a towering mass of thunderheads almost directly overhead. They seemed to have materialized out of nothing. At once it was cooler. But the wind had died almost completely.

"How's that feel?" he asked Topaz.

She smiled wanly at him, then turned back around to concentrate on the terrain ahead.

A moment later thunder rumbled like the booming of distant cannon. Slocum glanced up. The cumulus was building with amazing swiftness, and it had darkened considerably. In its restless, unfolding inner vaults, he saw lightning flickering. Slocum's dun flattened his ears as the mutter of the thunder came to him. He patted its neck to calm it and felt the stir of wind upon his neck. Abruptly the dun's mane was streaming straight ahead. Not long after came the first few large, scattered drops of rain.

"Better dig out your slicker!" he called to Topaz.

She nodded and tried to reach back.

He saw at once it was impossible. "Hold up. I'll get it," he told her.

She reined in her horse, then sagged wearily forward in her saddle as he dismounted swiftly, pulled her slicker out of her bedroll, and handed it up to her. She had some difficulty getting both arms through the slicker. But he was patient and a moment later he had slipped into his own slicker and was about to mount up again when he glanced back the way they had come.

A line of horsemen split the horizon. They were

closing fast, a plume of dust kicking up behind them. There was no need to wonder who they were. Apaches of the Moon Dog Lodge of the Mescaleros. They were evidently anxious to avenge the murder of their chieftain, Naratena.

"Topaz!" he said. "Look behind you!"

She turned—and appeared to shrivel inside her slicker. He stepped into his saddle, glancing up at the darkening sky as he did. The thunderhead was building, but the rain still fell in big, scattered drops, as if the gods of the storm were not yet sure if they should open the spigots all the way. The storm could still pass over harmlessly, Slocum realized, leaving in its wake only these few large drops for the sun to suck up in minutes.

But Slocum was betting on a heavy downpour. Better yet, a cloudburst.

"Don't head west!" Slocum told Topaz. "Turn south!"

"Why?"

"Never mind!" he said, glancing back again at the Apaches. "Follow me!"

He spurred his dun past her. Looking back, he saw she was keeping up with him. Abruptly, the wind came, heavier this time, like a palpable hand pushing at him. And then came the rain, the sound it made beating on the ground as it overtook them rising to a frightening crescendo. The gods had decided. The rain struck with a violence and suddenness that almost took Slocum's breath away. The dun stumbled slightly, but kept its head up and plunged on. Thunder boomed and lightning snapped. He glanced back. Topaz was still with him.

The rain lashed at them even harder, flailing at them with maddening insistence. Heavy, rain-laden wind squalls washed over them. Already Slocum was sore from the pounding his back was taking. He turned in his saddle to look back at Topaz. This time he could barely make her out.

"Turn!" he cried. "Swing west!"

As he called to her, he swung west. She caught his movement, even if she could not hear him above the roar of the storm, and followed him. Now they were moving with the wind and rain at their back and were able to make better time.

The tendrils of rain seemed almost solid ropes as they swept back and forth across the land, whipping and tearing at them. The sound the driving rain made as it pounded into the earth seemed to have increased in volume, and was almost as frightening as the cease-less crashing of the thunder and the searing, crackling tendrils of lightning that played about them. The ground by this time was soggy and treacherous under the dun's feet. Gleaming fingers of rock loomed out of the rain. They were nearing the canyons, Slocum re-alized.

He looked back, past Topaz. They gray veil of rain was like a curtain that had fallen between them and the rest of the world. There was no sign of the Apaches, nothing but the roaring wall of rain through which they raced.

An arroyo opened up before him. Slocum had been expecting this and did not hesitate. He put the dun down the bank, then waited for Topaz. When she reached him, he caught the reins of her horse and led it through the arroyo and out into a canyon that was already swirling with muddy water. Then he led Topaz back up the side of the canyon until he found a narrow ledge under a sheltering overhang of rock, close in under the rim. They were a good thirty yards or more, he judged, above the floor of the canyon by that time. He was gambling it would be high enough.

Dismounting, he helped Topaz from her saddle. She looked at him with a question in her eyes, but did not speak. She was too far gone for that. He carried her to the most level spot he could find under the overhang. Then he took off his slicker and placed it on the ground for her. She slumped onto it. He quickly unsaddled, took a blanket from his bedroll, and covered her with it. Then he tethered the horses to some scrub pine clinging to the canyon's slope and hunkered down beside Topaz to wait.

The rain still pelted him, and the lighning seemed to be probing the canyon for them, while the constant thunder seemed intent on blasting them out of their meager cover.

And then he heard it: the roar of water sweeping through the canyon toward them. He looked up the canyon and saw a wall of water charging through the downpour. The floodwaters were carrying great logs on their crest and thundering boulders were bounding along as well, like loose cannonballs. Caught between the canyon walls as between the sides of a chute, the rolling wall of brown water surged past, its swirling tendrils reaching almost as high as the ledge upon which Slocum and Topaz were perched.

The storm continued for a while longer. How long, it was difficult to tell. All sense of time and distance had been beaten out of them. Like dumb things they watched the torrent sweep past them, felt the thunder rock the ground under them, and tried not to notice the lightning.

At last, perhaps an hour or so later, the thunder abated somewhat and the lightning flickered less insistently. It was not long after that the roaring rain became only a steady, insistent downpour. The canyon below was still a turgid, roaring cataract, but it seemed to Slocum that the water was not as high as it had been.

He left Topaz and climbed to the rim of the canyon. He could see some distance now. Not an Apache was in sight. They were probably still going south, if they had not already turned off and headed back. The rain had completely obliterated any tracks they might have left, and in that furious downpour they could not have seen Slocum and Topaz turn off.

He turned and climbed back down to Topaz.

She was very weak and he had to sling her over his shoulder and carry her up to the rim. He laid her down reluctantly on the sopping ground, then went back to get the horses. It was obvious by now that he would have to carry her in front of him on his saddle and lead her horse.

She was able to help some as he pulled her up onto his pommel. He kept one arm around her and used his right hand to hold the reins, having already tied her pony's reins to the saddle horn. In this fashion they rode through the rain as swiftly as they could. The dun was tired, but no longer parched, and the animal seemed as anxious to keep going as they were. Like them, the horse wanted shelter from this brutal rain.

It was night when they reached Coppertown. Since sundown, Topaz had ridden with her head slumped back against Slocum's chest. The only evidence that she still lived came from the fever Slocum could feel raging within her.

It was still raining. The tin roofs on the shacks gleamed in the rain and the adobe buildings squatted like mushrooms in a damp cellar. Before he put his horse down the slope toward the town, however, Topaz stirred herself enough to direct him northeast, to a valley where Blucher had built himself a small shack.

It was dark when he saw the shack below him through the rain, nestled in the crook of a hill. He rode into the small valley and, swinging down, carried Topaz to the door. Turning his back to it, he rammed the door open and carried her into the cabin. It was roomy and dry inside.

He put her down on a bed in the far corner, then went back outside to tend to the horses. There was a lean-to that served as a stable in back of the shack. He off-saddled the horses and crowded them into it, then found a feed bag and some grain under a wooden trough and put the feed bag on his dun, promising himself he'd take care of Topaz's pony later.

Inside, he shucked out of his slicker, took wood from a pile of mesquite roots, and built a fire in the fireplace. The fire caught, the flames leaped, and the room grew warm. He went over to see to Topaz.

She was not conscious. Carefully, he lifted her slender body with his big hands and unwound the bloody bandage to inspect her wound. It was worse, so much worse that when he saw it, he felt sick and turned away. Doing his best to make her comfortable, he stood back and looked down at her, trying to remember the name of that doctor she had mentioned.

After a minute, her words came to him clearly, as if she had been standing beside him, fully conscious. The doctor was a man who had death in his eyes. They called him Lucifer Garrett.

Slocum went down on one knee beside Topaz. Even though he knew she could not hear him, he said, "I'm going into Coppertown, Topaz. I'll bring that Lucifer fellow out to fix you up. Hang on."

He built up the fire some, then left.

The lights of Coppertown gleamed brightly as he rode toward them. The rain had ended finally, and the air was miraculously cool, washed clean and clear. What stars were visible through the broken racks of clouds seemed incredibly close and bright, as if they were being observed through spectacles. Thunder still muttered in the foothills behind the town and a few dark cloud masses overhead occasionally flared with distant lightning.

Riding onto Coppertown's main street, he found it fetlock-deep in clinging mud. The unpainted buildings looked bedraggled. The rain barrels were all overflowing and some gutters had been carried away by the force of the storm. They hung now from the edges of roofs, some with their ends dug solidly into the ground.

Slocum pulled up in front of the livery, dismounted, and led his dun into it. An old man with a light thatch of red hair came out of a feed room, saw him, and leaned his pitchfork against the side of a stall.

"Go light on the oats," Slocum told him as he let the dun walk toward him. "But give him a good rub-down."

"That'll be two bits, mister."

Slocum flipped a coin at him. The old man snatched the coin out of the air with the quickness of a striking snake.

"Where can I find Lucifer Garrett?" Slocum asked.

"Try Latimer's Barber Shop. Or Steadman's. More'n likely he's in The Gold Nugget, drunk or playin' cards."

Slocum nodded and strode from the livery. He didn't bother with the barbershop or Steadman's; he went directly to The Gold Nugget. Bellying up to the bar, he ordered a whiskey and looked around. This late, the saloon was almost empty, except for a couple of miners in a corner conversing over their bottles and three more at a table playing poker.

One other patron was against the wall in the back, slumped forward onto his table. The dim light of the place did not carry that far and it was impossible for Slocum to get any idea of what the man looked like, except for the fact that he was dressed in a dark frock coat and trousers. Slocum guessed this gent might be Garrett, but he wanted to make sure.

Slocum pulled his bottle toward him and poured himself a drink. The bartender was watching him covertly, aware of the fact that he was a stranger in town and, from the look of him, not a miner.

Slocum beckoned the barkeep closer. "I was told I might find Dr. Garrett here," Slocum said.

"Doctor?" The barkeep was amused. He was a tall fellow with a greased mustache, heavy in the shoulders, and with eyes a little too close together. "You mean Lucifer, don't you?"

"Perhaps I do, at that."

The barkeep pointed to the fellow in the frock coat. "Lucifer's over there, sleeping it off. He got an early start today." He grinned. "About twelve noon."

Slocum paid for his drink, downed his whiskey, and strode over to the table where Lucifer Garrett was resting. The stench of sour whiskey hung over the man like a curse, and Slocum felt his heart sink when he realized that this man represented whatever hope he had that Topaz would live out the night.

Slocum bent and shook Garrett by the shoulder, without gentleness, insistently, until at last the man raised his head in protest and glared foggily up at Slocum.

"Go 'way," he muttered. "See me later... barbershop."

Before Garrett could lower his head again, Slocum slapped him hard. Garrett's eyes flew open in sudden, startled pain. He pulled back quickly, then looked closer at Slocum.

"Damn you, mister! See me later! I'll be up and about soon."

He started to put his head down again. Before he could, however, Slocum grabbed his shirtfront and hauled him roughly to his feet. Then he glanced back at the barkeep. "You got any coffee?" he asked.

"Take more'n coffee to sober up Lucifer," the barkeep snorted.

"I asked you a question, mister."

"Across the street. Ma's restaurant is still open if you knock loud enough and long enough."

Aroused now, though still unsteady on his feet, Garrett tried to pull out of Slocum's grasp, but Slocum pulled him along as one would an idiot child. As Garrett stumbled past the bar, he reached out and grabbed hold of it with sudden tenacity. Slocum had to pull up. When he did, Garrett tore himself out of Slocum's grasp, and before Slocum could blink an eye, Garrett had drawn a short-barreled Colt from a shoulder rig.

Slocum had not expected this, and was taken completely by surprise. He took a step back. Behind him he heard chuckles. Excited talk from the low porch in front of the saloon indicated it was already crowded with townsmen and miners come to watch.

Lucifer Garrett had dark, neatly combed hair and gray eyes. His face was thin, hollow-cheeked, and as pale as alabaster. He looked like Death in a frock coat. Though he must have been close to one hundred proof, judging from the alcoholic waves emanating from his person, he held the Colt with the steadiness of a rock.

Garrett shook his head quickly to rid himself of any remaining cobwebs. "Now, damn you, mister, who are you, and what in Hades do you want of me? Can't you see I am drunk? My faculties are clouded. As a physician I am useless."

"My name's Slocum. John Slocum. I got a sick woman. She's been sliced, bad. Since last night. Right now she's running a fever."

"A knife wound?"

"Yes."

"A knife used in hunting, I suppose? Not cleaned— not a kitchen knife, say?"

"No. Not a kitchen knife."

With a sigh, Garrett straightened up and holstered his Colt. "I will go with you," he said. "But I hope, for your sake, that you realize how poor the prognosis is in such cases."

"Just do what you can," Slocum said.

"Of course."

Garrett strode closer to Slocum and slapped him hard. Slocum's head whipped around. Taking a step back, he resisted the impulse to hold his hand up to his burning cheek. Though Garrett had swung with all the force he could muster, Slocum had been in no danger of going down.

"In better days," Garrett said, almost wistfully, "you would have gone down, mister."

"I am sure of it. Could we ride out now? We can take care of this matter between us later."

"I would be delighted to give you satisfaction, sir. But, as you say, later. First, however, I am very much afraid I will need that coffee." Even as Garrett spoke, he sagged forward.

Slocum had to jump quickly to catch him. As Slocum helped him from the saloon, the doctor chuckled and told Slocum that he found it difficult to walk when the floor kept rushing up at him.

"You have no idea how difficult it was to keep that gun steady," Garrett went on, "with the saloon whirling about my head."

"I'm just grateful you *did* keep it steady," Slocum replied, pushing through the watching crowd and heading across the street to Ma's Restaurant.

* * *

Garrett was sober enough by the time they reached the cabin. The fire in the fireplace had almost gone out, but that didn't matter much to Topaz. She was still on fire, as Garrett verified.

Slocum lit some kerosene lamps he found lying about and soon Garrett had sufficient light.

"Boil some water," Garrett told Slocum as he proceeded to examine Topaz's wound.

By the time Slocum had found the outside water pump and managed to heat the water in a large iron pot he hung in the fireplace, a considerable amount of time had passed, and Garrett was visibly distressed. Before riding out with Slocum, he had stepped into his office at the rear of the barbershop to pick up his black bag, some cotton bandages, and a bottle of whiskey. Slocum had not been happy to see Garrett emerge from his office with the bottle of whiskey and had decided that if Garrett took as much as a single swig from the bottle he would smash it from his hand. But the man had placed the bottle in his saddlebag and left it there. Now, as Slocum watched the man work, he knew why.

Dipping the cloth bandages he had brought with him into the steaming water, Garrett added liberal dollops of whiskey and then began scrubbing at the long gash. Fresh bleeding broke out almost at once. Though Topaz remained unconscious, she began tossing fretfully as Garrett scrubbed away at her wound with an almost brutal thoroughness.

When Garrett had the entire slash wide open once again, the ragged, gaping lips of the wound blood red and pulsing with blood, Slocum had to turn away. Garrett appeared to know what he was doing, but it was hard to understand why opening Topaz up like this was going to help.

"Boil some more water," Garrett told him.

"What the hell are you trying to do? Turn her inside out, for Christ's sake?"

"For Topaz's sake, I am trying to clean out her wound. When I am sure it is clean, I will close it. I wish I had maggots or leeches. Some Indians have found a mold they use. As it is, I must rely on hot water and whiskey and this girl's naturally tough disposition. Now, will you please boil more water, or must I do it myself?"

Slocum picked up the wooden bucket and went outside for more water.

6

About a week later, a little before sundown, Slocum and Topaz were sitting on makeshift stools in front of the shack when Lucifer Garrett rode up. They were surprised to see him. After his visit the day before, he had told Topaz he would not need to check on her again until the end of the week.

Slocum stood up as Garrett dismounted and led his horse toward them. As usual, Garrett looked as if he had not slept much the night before, which was more than likely the case. As Garrett had explained to them, if a man could not sleep for coughing and fever, he might as well go downstairs and play cards and have himself a few belts. What was the difference, he asked, if the burning was in the gut or in the chest? It all came to the same thing in the end.

"This is a surprise," said Topaz, smiling. She was still pale and had lost some weight, but she was getting much of her old spirit back and, as Slocum had noticed of late, was eating like a famished wolf. "Did you leave something? You said you wouldn't be back for a while."

Garrett pulled to a stop before her and brushed his long, pale fingers nervously down the sides of his trousers. Then he took off his black, flat-crowned Stetson and looked somewhat unhappily at them both. "I didn't think I'd be coming back this soon, either, Topaz."

"What is it, Garrett?" Slocum asked.

"Trouble, the way I see it. But maybe I'm wrong," the doctor replied.

"Speak clear," Slocum urged.

"Two men rode in last night. I met them in The Gold Nugget this afternoon."

"What about them?" Topaz asked.

"They were asking questions about Topaz and you, Slocum."

"Describe them," said Slocum.

"They made quite a pair. One of them was wearing a greasy eye patch, but he made no little real effort to keep the damn thing down over his empty eye socket. His face had been injured fearfully, my guess is when he was quite young. A kick from a horse, maybe."

Topaz shuddered. "Mat Wall," she said, her voice low and troubled.

"The other one was the leanest fellow I ever saw. He had long gray hair and was all elbows and knees, but he looked as hard as greasewood."

"That would be Ben Stringfellow," said Slocum.

"You say there were just the two of them?" Topaz asked.

"That's right."

Topaz and Slocum exchanged glances. Slocum looked back at Garrett. "There should be two others: Shorty and Slate Cadey. One of them I winged in the shoulder, the other I had to crunch on the head. The last we saw of them, they were hog-tied real proper by Topaz here and left in a mine shaft in the Superstitions."

"They didn't say anything about any others. They appear to be acting alone."

"So what's the problem?" Slocum asked.

"They been talking," Garrett said.

"About what?"

"The Dutchman's mine. The one that kept Jacob Waltz alive all these years. They've been mentioning a map. They say they bought it from Blucher, but before he could deliver it to them, Topaz hired you to kill Blucher and take the map from him."

"A filthy lie!" Topaz snapped, getting to her feet.

Slocum glanced sardonically at Garrett. "Did they say how they knew all this? What were they supposed to have been doing while we were do busy—standing around watching?"

"Of course no one bothers to ask such questions, Slocum. What matters is that they have succeeded in convincing some old friends of Blucher that this is exactly what happened."

"But they know about me and Amos!" Topaz said. "How could they think I would do such a thing to that old man?"

"Give a man enough liquor," Slocum reminded her, "and he'll find considerable pleasure in believing just about anything."

"Especially if it gives him a chance to vent his natural meanness in the process," Garrett agreed, his mouth a thin, grim line.

"I'll saddle up," said Slocum. "Go in there for a word with them two."

"I'll go with you," said Topaz.

"No, you won't. You'll stay with Garrett. I'll want him to keep an eye on things in case a few of Blucher's old buddies decide to come out here to express their indignation." Slocum turned to Garrett. "Will you do that for me, Garrett? Will you stay here with Topaz?"

"Of course, Slocum. But I don't like the idea of you going into Coppertown alone."

"Don't like it myself, but I don't see as I got much choice in the matter. Besides, it'll be dark by the time I get there, and I'll see to it that I have a surprise or two up my sleeve when I do meet up with them."

He hurried to the stalls in back to saddle his dun. A moment later, as he rode around to the front of the shack, Topaz walked out to say goodbye to him. He bent and stroked her raven hair.

"It's gettin' chilly," he told her. "Go inside and feed the fire some. But keep an eye out."

"Yes."

She pulled him down so he could kiss her on the

lips. She had never done a thing like that with him before. It was a gentle, very human thing to do, and it touched him deeply. He was seeing more and more of the white woman in her as the days passed. Yet it was good to know as well what real passion seethed just below that surprising gentleness.

He waved to Garrett and rode out.

As Slocum had predicted, it was dark when he reached Coppertown. He did not take the road that led into it from the mine above the town. Instead, he kept to the hills and rode past the town, then cut down toward the backside of Coppertown, avoiding the wooden plank bridge and splashing through the creek instead. He came up out of the creek behind Main Street and dismounted, tethering his horse to the back porch railing of a feed store.

Passing through an alley, Slocum came out on the main street and kept against the storefronts as he moved down to The Gold Nugget. Pushing through the saloon's batwings, he paused and looked the place over. As soon as the saloon's patrons saw him standing there, the long, smoke-filled room went almost perfectly quiet. A laughing Mexican girl sitting on a customer's lap in the back had to be hushed into silence.

One glance about the place and Slocum knew that neither Mat Wall nor Ben Stringfellow was in there. Slocum strode toward the bar. Elbowing a few gawking miners aside, he bought cigars and a bottle of whiskey and took them over to a table in a corner, poured himself a shot, downed it, then thumbed a lucifer to life and lit his cigar.

It wasn't long before a miner eased himself toward the door, then darted out through the batwings. The sound of the little man's running feet grew softer as Slocum poured himself another drink. After a few moments he asked the bartender for a deck of cards. As soon as the deck was brought, he pulled his table closer, shifted the Navy Colt from his belt to the top of his thigh just behind his knee, then began his game of solitaire. Lifting his boot heel slightly, he was able to keep the Colt perfectly level and well out of sight. All this he did in one smooth, continuous motion. Not a soul in the saloon caught it.

Gradually, as he got engrossed in his game, the level of sound in the saloon came up a bit, though it never reached the level it had been at when Slocum first stepped through the batwings. It was not long before Slocum became aware of a careful, hushed commotion outside the saloon. Pretending he heard nothing, he continued to slap the cards down before him, checking his hole cards every now and then.

He heard the sudden silence and the batwings flipping shut and looked up. Mat Wall and Ben Stringfellow were standing in front of the door. A discreet but swift evacuation of the front part of the saloon took place.

"Heard you got out of that mine shaft," Slocum told them.

"No thanks to you," Wall said.

"No thanks wanted. What happened to Shorty—and Slate?"

"Slate died. That gunshot of yours killed him. And Shorty never had a chance. The whole place caved in on him before we could get him out."

"That's too bad," Slocum said.

"You planned it that way."

Slocum smiled and began to pick up his hand. "Let's just say I was hoping."

"We're going to kill you, Slocum."

"All by yourself?" Slocum palmed the full deck of cards and placed them down on the table, his hand resting on its edge.

Mat Wall smiled, with that part of his face that could. Ben Stringfellow took a couple of quick steps to the side.

"No," Wall said. "We want to be sure we kill you—before we go after that bitch of a half-breed who sold out poor old Blucher."

These words were intended to enrage Slocum and cause him to make the first move. When they didn't, Slocum saw Wall's face become just a shade paler.

In as mild a tone as he could manage, Slocum said, "You know that's bullshit. Topaz loved that old man, and when I came along you had both of them digging in that damned mine. And something you should know, Wall: there was no gold in that mine. That wasn't the Dutchman's mine. Blucher just led you to that one to put you off the trail. He and Topaz knew you were following them before they were ten miles out of here."

"That's a damned lie!"

"No, it isn't, Wall. And that makes you the bastard responsible for Amos Blucher's death, even if it was Slate who pulled the trigger."

Wall shifted his head to look at Ben. The movement took only a second, but it was all Slocum needed. His hand dropped to his thigh, and before Wall's hog-leg cleared leather, Slocum's Navy Colt was thundering from under the table. Leaping to his feet, Slocum flung the table at Ben Stringfellow, then continued to fire at Wall.

Smoke obscured Wall's figure. The man staggered back, firing wildly, then turned and plunged back out through the saloon door. Ben Stringfellow was fighting off the table and never did get his weapon out all the way before Slocum turned on him and punched two quick holes in his narrow gut.

As Stringfellow collapsed to the floor, Slocum turned and pushed his way through the packed mass of patrons at the rear of the saloon, and darted out into the back alley.

The last Slocum had seen of Wall, he was heading north, toward the bridge. Slocum took that direction, too, hoping to cut him off. He hadn't meant to let the man get away like this and was furious with himself. Wall should have been hit more than once, but obviously he was unscathed. Ducking down an alley, Slocum heard someone running down Main Street toward him.

He flattened himself against a wall and watched the running figure cross the head of the alley. It could be Wall. The size of the man was right. Slocum left the alley and started down the sidewalk after him, then abruptly pulled up. He was not chasing Wall, but a tall youngster. The kid was probably just running home to tell his folks about the gunfight.

Slocum turned, his heart suddenly pounding. He was out in the middle of a moonlit street, in plain sight. He hurried back into the mouth of the alley he had just left and peered back up the street in the direction the tall kid had taken. He saw nothing but the dim shapes of buildings huddled in the darkness. Had Wall got that far already?

The sound of hooves came suddenly. He turned. Up the alley he had just left swept Wall, heading directly toward him. Slocum flung up his gun hand and fired, then dove to one side. He was not fast enough. The horse drove into him, knocking him viciously to one side. Then he was down, rolling, his gun flying out of his hand. He grabbed for his .44, and that was the last thing he remembered as his head struck the corner of something hard and unyielding.

Wall was not unscathed. One of Slocum's rounds had caught him in the side, and his right boot was already heavy with blood. But with Slocum out of the way now, only Topaz remained between him and that Dutchman's mine.

He rode hard, not allowing his wound to slow him. He simply would not think about it. Just as he had never allowed himself to think about what his old man's Percheron had done to him. His old man had told him a hundred times afterward that he had simply not known Mat was standing in the corner of the horse stall, watching. And of course there was no reason why he should think a ten-year-old would do such a fool thing. So when that damn Percheron had started kicking, there had been nothing his Pa could do to help him. In his mind's eye, Wall saw once again, through a livid, exploding veil of blood, his father's anguished face bending close.

No, Wall would not think about it. Just as he would not think about this growing hole in his side. He would think instead of the gold, of what it would purchase for him. He would move to San Francisco and buy all the women he wanted, and when he took them, he would take off his patch and make them pretend they saw nothing.

Yes. That was what he would do.

He was on the crest of a ridge now, the pass leading into Blucher's valley visible against the starlit sky. He bent low over his mount and scoured its sides with his rowels.

Slocum blinked his eyes and looked up at the crowd gathering around him. It was clear they thought he had been killed by Mat Wall and were trying to decide what to do with him.

He sat up and felt of his head. There was a laceration along the back of his skull where he had struck the corner of the building. Nothing serious. He would live. His .44 was beside him. He holstered it and scrambled to his feet and started looking for his Navy Colt. At once a miner stepped forward and handed it to him.

"You all right, Slocum?" the man asked.

Slocum nodded and stuck the revolver into his belt.

"Is that true what you said back there, that it was Slate who killed old Amos Blucher?"

"Yes. It was Slate Cadey who shot Blucher," Slocum said.

"Damn," the miner said, rubbing his hand along a stubbled cheek.

"How long have I been out?"

"Not long."

"How long, damn it!" Slocum snapped.

"About five minutes, I'd say. We . . . didn't know

what to do, you layin' there, an' all . . ."

Slocum did not wait for him to finish. He whirled and ran back down through the alley to the rear of the feed store where he had tethered his dun. As he rode out of town, he did not spare his mount. Wall had a dangerously long head start on him, and Slocum knew precisely where the son of a bitch was heading.

Fortunately, he had not left Topaz alone.

He saw what must have been Wall's horse tethered in a draw behind the shack. Swiftly dismounting, he angled down the slope to the shack and peered in the bedroom window. He could see through the small room into the main room. Topaz was sitting at the kitchen table. Garrett was sitting across from her. They were playing cards, for Christ's sake!

That meant Wall was still out here somewhere, getting ready to make his move. Slocum looked quickly around, but he could see nothing about him in the mist-shrouded valley. The moon had already dropped below the hills. The bastard could be anywhere. The only thing Slocum could do was warn Topaz and Garrett, then get Topaz the hell out of here. He hurried around to the front of the shack and entered.

Topaz and Garrett turned. What he saw on their faces warned him, but not in time. He felt the muzzle of Wall's rifle dig deep into his side and heard the man's ugly laugh. Turning, he saw Wall step out from behind the door. To Slocum's surprise, he saw that Wall was wounded. A dark shield of blood extended down his thigh all the way into his boots. But the wound and the loss of blood did not seem to hamper the man.

"Drop that gun you got in your belt, Slocum," he

said, "and the other one in your cross-draw rig. Reach in nice and slow, now."

Slocum dropped both weapons to the floor.

"I should kill you," Wall said, kicking both weapons into a corner, "but Topaz said if I did that, she would never tell me where the mine was, no matter what I did to her. And she's an Apache, so I believe her."

"She still won't tell you." Slocum stepped all the way in and kicked the door shut behind him.

"Yes, she will," Wall sneered. "When she sees me start picking you apart with this rifle, she will. And all I want is for her to make the map clearer."

"He made me show it to him, Slocum," Topaz said. "I knew it wouldn't do him any good."

"Forget it, Topaz," Slocum said.

"Sorry I couldn't warn you," said Garrett. "He heard you come riding over the ridge."

"Never mind," said Slocum. "I should have been more careful."

He started to turn to face Wall, but Wall shoved the barrel viciously into Slocum's side. Flinching away, Slocum stumbled awkwardly toward the table. As he put his hands out to catch himself, Garrett jumped to his feet, a Colt materializing in his hand. It blazed once, the round catching Wall high on his left shoulder and slamming him back against the wall. But before Garrett could fire again, Mat Wall had pumped two quick shots into Garrett's chest.

Slocum flung himself toward Wall, but the man was already bolting back out through the door. As Slocum charged after him, a rifle shot came from the darkness and a piece of the doorjamb disintegrated.

Slocum ducked back inside the shack, and a moment later came the sudden hoofbeats of Wall's horse as he rode off.

Turning back to Garrett, Slocum saw at once that the man's wounds were fatal. Garrett, however, refused to lie back on the cot. He insisted on sitting up. For a dying man, he seemed astonishingly alive, his eyes gleaming with expectation. It was almost too much for Slocum, and for Topaz as well.

At last Garrett began to lose consciousness for longer and longer periods and could no longer sit up on the cot. Topaz made him as comfortable as she could, then knelt beside him while Slocum stood over the cot, looking down into the face of the man who had death in his eyes. Momentarily regaining consciousness, Garrett smiled up at him. "I am afraid I will not be able to give you satisfaction for that slap, after all, Slocum," he said.

"Perhaps some other time."

"Yes, some other time."

"In a better place than this."

"Most assuredly," Garrett murmured.

Topaz began to weep.

Slocum cleared his throat and forced himself to say something. "Where in blazes did you get that revolver, Garrett? Didn't Wall disarm you?"

"I was expecting trouble so I secreted Topaz's weapon in my belt, in the small of my back."

"I'm sorry, Garrett."

"Do not weep for me, Slocum. Nor you, Topaz. Life is for the living, not for the living dead. The sentence was passed on me a long time ago, but a cold and capricious fate had denied that it be carried out in full. So I lingered, waiting for that shadowy gentleman to step out of the corner finally and pluck at my sleeve. He has come for me at last. My curse has been lifted. You do understand, don't you?"

Her head still bowed, Topaz nodded.

Slocum took a deep breath. "Yes," he said, "I understand."

"Good. Then I want a celebration when you plant me. For it will be a joyous occasion."

Abruptly, Topaz jumped to her feet and ran outside.

"That's a hell of a thing," said Slocum, trying to ignore the ache in his throat, "making an Indian cry."

Garrett frowned slightly. "I will miss her. You take good care of her. Maybe this business with the gold . . . you should forget?"

"We'll see."

"Of course. I am no one to give advice."

He began to cough then. Topaz heard it from outside and hurried back in. She had regained her composure.

Slocum pulled up a chair and the three of them talked quietly until the first light of dawn showed on the tops of the hills. As daylight streamed into the valley, Garrett said goodbye to both of them and very quietly and peacefully died.

Late that morning, Topaz and Slocum buried Garrett on a hillock overlooking the cabin. Topaz had selected the site herself. In keeping with Garrett's request, they tried to make it a celebration, but they were not very successful in doing so.

As they returned to the cabin, Topaz looked back

up at the gravesite and frowned. "First Amos Blucher," she said, "and now Lucifer Garrett. This gold—I think it is accursed."

"Not the gold, only those who have the fever for it."

"But are there any white eyes who do not?" she asked.

Slocum shrugged. "Garrett wondered if maybe we shouldn't just forget about it."

"It is easy for me to forget it, Slocum. I am Apache. But the fever, it still burns in you, does it not?"

"I suppose it does. I'm human, like anyone else. I can imagine what wealth could do for me," he said.

"Or *to* you," she replied.

"Yes, I suppose that's so."

"Slocum, it is not for me that I want this gold," Topaz told him.

Slocum pulled up and looked down at Topaz. "Maybe you better explain that."

"It is for The People that Blucher and I tried to find the mine."

"The People? I thought the Apache could not catch gold fever."

"They must catch it. They have no choice. With this gold they can buy rifles, repeating rifles, and all the bullets they need. And later, maybe, the wagon guns."

"But who would sell that kind of weaponry to Apaches?"

She smiled then. "I have been long enough with the whites to know that there is always someone to give the Apache what he wants if the Apache has gold. If the Apache has this gold, there will be someone to sell the Apache all the weapons he needs."

Topaz was absolutely correct. If the price was right—and solid gold was a right fair price—then there would be gun dealers aplenty flocking into the Superstition Mountains to sell their wares to the Apaches. No law in the world could banish greed.

"And you say Blucher was going along with you on this?" Slocum asked.

"He liked the Apache, Slocum. And he understood, as I do now, that The People's time in this land is nearly at an end."

"Then what's the sense?"

They were inside the shack by that time. Topaz slumped down at the table. She looked drawn. She was not yet completely recovered, and the excitement of the past few hours had left her shaky. She looked wearily up at Slocum.

"What is the sense? Time! It will give the Apache a little more time, perhaps."

"And that's enough?"

"Yes, Slocum. That is enough, because The People can hope for nothing better."

Slocum nodded and sat down across from Topaz. He smiled at her. She was right. The Apaches would fight simply to last as long as they could. Sure as hell, they knew they must lose in the end. But what did that matter? To die well—that was the only thing that counted.

Slocum recalled that poor son of a bitch Tate Rawson. The Apaches had punished him as they had because a man who would die like that frightened them. In that screaming, crawling excuse for a man, they saw what was possible—not only for the white eyes, but just possibly for themselves as well.

And if this were so, it would be the end of the Apache.

"So you want to give this gold mine to the Apaches."

She nodded. "To The People."

"Not for 'your' people."

"I have none. I live between people. I am a half-breed. I belong not in one world or the other."

Slocum got up and pulled Topaz gently to her feet. Then he kissed her just as gently. She snaked her arms up around his neck and rested her head against his chest. Without a word, they turned and went into the little bedroom.

There really wasn't that much difference between them, Slocum figured. Both of them lived between worlds. He had left one world to go to war, and he was still looking for another to take its place.

He looked down at Topaz and smiled. As soon as her head had struck the bed, she had fallen asleep. It was not what he had been thinking of when he took her hand and led her in here, and he was sure this had not been her intention, either. Gently, so as not to awaken her, he pulled a blanket over her and walked softly out of the room.

It was just as well. He had some thinking to do.

7

The matter of the Dutchman's mine did not come up again immediately. Topaz did a lot of sleeping, and for his part, Slocum took it easy for the first time in a long, long time. He was enjoying himself hugely. It was, in fact, the first holiday he had ever given himself.

A week almost to the day after Lucifer Garrett's death, Slocum entered the shack with a fresh load of firewood and proceeded to build up the fire. It was not long before the fireplace was thundering. The heavy, aromatic warmth of the wood fire filled the small cabin. He stood up and took a step back, gazing reflectively down at his handiwork. Man, the bringer of fire. Hell, before long, he would be leaning back in a rocker, smoking a pipe.

He heard a light step behind him.

Turning, he found Topaz standing inches from him. She was wearing a smile and no more.

"I am much better," she said. "See?"

He looked. And she was right. A long red line, broader in some places than in others, was all that remained of Naratena's ugly slash. The wound was almost completely healed. But it was not this fact that had the sweat standing out on his forehead.

She understood at once what he was going through, and smiled impishly. "Some time ago," she said, stepping into his arms, "we started something we didn't finish. I fell asleep, did I not?"

"Yes."

"And you covered me with a warm blanket and left the room."

"It seemed like the best thing to do at the time," Slocum said.

"I am better now. I am no longer sleepy and you have filled the cabin with warmth." She stepped back and took his hand. "Why don't we finish now what we started then?"

"You sure you're up to it?"

"Try me."

Until this moment he had not shared her bed, having slept on the cot in the main room. He had been a very considerate—and very proper—man. Now she made him sit on the edge of the bed while she undressed him. She had gained back most if not all of the weight she had lost earlier, and in just the last few days, it seemed, had become once again that full-bodied creature of lush curves and sheer animal magnetism he had known before. Twice that day he had found it extremely difficult to keep from reaching out and pulling her to him.

But now when he went to touch or kiss her, she slapped his hands away and made him sit still. She knew what she was doing. By the time she pushed his naked body back down onto the bed, he was on fire. It was a warmth evidently matched by her own as she flung herself eagerly upon him and plunged her mouth down upon his, her wanton tongue probing deeply, hungrily. Pulling back after a moment, she fastened her teeth firmly but gently about his upper lip and began to tease it.

Her aim, obviously, was to drive him wild, and she was succeeding. Chuckling softly, Slocum pulled back, then rolled her off him, so that they were facing each other. Thrusting her hand boldly, insistently between his thighs, Topaz found that he was ready for her. With a delighted laugh, she grasped his erection with a strength that almost made him cry out.

"See!" she cried triumphantly. "See how strong I am! I am better! Much better."

He chuckled in agreement as she buried her face in the thick hair on his chest and began nibbling on one of his nipples. He was amazed at the effect this had on him. With a deep, guttural mutter of delight, he grabbed her firm buttocks and pulled her hard against him, then rolled over onto her.

She was ready as well. More than ready. She thrust

her thighs up with an almost angry urgency, and he felt the tip of his erection probing the moist entrance to her womb. She cried out and thrust her thighs up still higher, then wrapped both legs about his waist. He plunged deeply into her and gasped in pleasure as he felt how tightly the muscles of her vagina held him. Soon the mindless rhythm of his thrusting caused him to lose all sense of time. Topaz, too, was caught up in the wild frenzy of their coupling. She began turning her head rapidly from side to side, her eyes shut tightly, swearing steadily in a mixture of Spanish and Apache that sent a delicious shiver up his back.

And that was what did it for him. With a grim, wild plunge he drove down into her, impaling her with a ferocity that matched her own. He felt her shudder convulsively under him as she let out a prolonged scream that was more like a wail of terror. It sent shock waves of desire through him and he began to come repeatedly, clinging to her fiercely, as progressively more violent climaxes convulsed them both. They grew fiercely into each other, becoming one flesh, a single, twisting, moaning entity. . . .

They had napped for a delicious while, clasped to each other, spinning off into a sweet sleep. Now they were awake again, and Slocum felt faint, lascivious echoes of their earlier lovemaking stirring to life once more within him. Lying on his side, his head propped on his palm, Slocum looked in wonder at Topaz.

Her long black hair hung over her face, partially obscuring one eye. She smiled, then reached over and down to his crotch. To his surprise, he found he was ready again. She flung her hair back over her shoulder and pushed herself closer to him.

"Now, I will ride you," she told him, nibbling his ear for a moment.

She pushed him over gently and slid up onto him like a snake, then lay there, her legs crossed tightly about his erection. Hungrily, she pressed her mouth hard down upon his, her tongue probing with an insistent, delicious wantonness that lit a fire in him clear down to his loins and caused him to writhe involuntarily under her. With a sudden, delighted laugh, she leaned swiftly back, pulled her legs forward, then drove herself down upon him with a violence he was afraid would injure her.

It did nothing of the sort. Gasping with pleasure, she began to pound on his chest and ride him like an Apache warrior, twisting and plunging, first forward, then sideways. He might have been a broomtail she was attempting to break. She began to come repeatedly. Each time she did, she let out a cry that was more like a sob. At last he found he could no longer keep himself from climaxing. The moment he let go, she felt his pulsating, thrusting orgasm and clung to him still more tightly, tightening her muscles about his shaft in a fierce effort to keep him erect.

It worked. Laughing exultantly, she began to move once more—steadily, slowly this time. His shaft probed so deeply at times that its tip seemed to be on fire. Still thrusting gently, she leaned away suddenly, still grinding herself gently down upon his erection, and flung her head back, seemingly drunk on the mystery and beauty of it. Slocum began to wonder if it would ever end—if, perhaps, they might not have crossed some threshold beyond which desire was never satisfied, where coupling became an end in itself, extending into a distant time, the only reality....

Abruptly, he found himself coming alive again, lifting to meet her every thrust. Suddenly he reached up to grab her thighs. Now it was his turn. He wanted her under him, to drive upon her once more, to plunge deeply, deeper than he had ever gone with her or with any other woman.

"Down!" he cried to her. "Down! I want you under me."

She just laughed with delight as he reached up and plucked her down off him, swept her in under him, then straddled her hungrily. This time there was no teasing, nothing but his total, devouring need to finish it—and finally he did, crushing her with his weight, lunging into her with a fierceness and a violence that astonished him.

Rolling off her at last, he felt almost ashamed, especially when he saw how pale she was, subdued even, as she lay on her back, face up beside him. He wondered then if he might have injured her somehow.

"Are you all right, Topaz?" he asked.

She turned her head to look at him. "Yes, John Slocum, I am all right. What did you think?"

"You were so quiet. I thought . . . I might have hurt you."

She smiled to comfort him. "It was a storm, John. We were both caught up in it. But it has passed now. For a moment I knew nothing, felt nothing. I had gone beyond to another place. My mother told me once how such a thing could happen when a man made love to a woman, but I had given up hope that I would ever be so lucky." She reached out and placed her hand on Slocum's cheek. "But I was wrong. And it was a white man, not an Apache, who did it for me. You are a strangely fierce yet gentle man, John Slocum."

Relieved, Slocum just nodded and let his eyes feast on her. She was quite a combination, he concluded, Spanish and Apache.

"Tell me about your mother, Topaz," he said.

"Her name was Rosaria."

"She was captured by the Apaches?"

"Yes. By my father, a warrior, who became the famous Apache chief, Emiliano."

"How old was she at the time she was captured?"

"Twenty-two."

"That's pretty late. Must have been hard for her to adjust."

"It was. My father captured her only a week before she was to be married to the son of a very wealthy landowner, a young man she had known for as long as she could remember. She had gone to Spain for her education and had been back in her home for only a few weeks when the Apaches raided her father's *estancia*. She never said much about the young man she was to marry, but I know she had loved him very much. In the locket she kept hidden from all but me there is an inscription that reads, 'To My Betrothed. Love, Julio.' It was around her neck when Emiliano captured her."

"Do you have it?"

"Yes. I still have it." Topaz sighed. "My mother did her best to become a good Apache and to be a loyal, faithful wife to her husband. But it was not easy for her. After my birth, Emiliano soon took other wives and for too long he would leave my mother's bed. But she was patient and never let me see what pain she felt. It was only later that I realized how very lonely she had been all those years."

"It is amazing she did as well as she did."

"Yes. It was only just before she died that I realized what luxuries she had enjoyed during her youth as the beloved only daughter of a rich *hidalgo*. At the end, she found it very hard to understand why her God had cast her aside, exiling her to this rude, cruel land and into the arms of a savage who could caress only children. Before she died, she told me to go to find my people. She was sure that if any of them were alive, they would take me in and give me a home."

"Did you find them?"

"I did not get beyond the border towns. And by that time I knew what I could expect. I am a half-breed, John Slocum. I told you before. I live between two worlds. I do not belong in the world of the white man or the world of the Apache."

"Don't talk like that."

"It is all right, John Slocum. You are the same, are you not? Where are your people? Where is your home?"

"It's not quite the same for me."

She looked at him searchingly for a long while. "No," she said at length, "it is not the same for you."

"Topaz, about the gold. I have been thinking."

"Ah! All that gold! I wondered when you would talk of it again."

"If we were to take enough for us, we could leave the mine for the Apaches, but would they let us back into the Superstition Mountains to reach the mine?"

"It would be dangerous. Very dangerous. But I am the daughter of a chief. And only I know where the mine is."

"They could not force you to tell them?"

Her eyes became darker, and the tiny lines about her mouth grew hard. In that instant she became an Apache once more. "I would not tell them a thing. They know that. You should know that, too, John Slocum."

He smiled. "I know that now. It was a foolish question, I suppose."

"Yes, it was." Then her face softened, and she leaned slightly closer. "Tell me, did I hear correctly? Did you not say, 'take enough for us'?"

"Yes. For us. We could settle down on a ranch somewhere in the high country. There's some good land left east of the Absarokas. You'd love it there, Topaz."

She looked at him for a long moment, incredulous.

"What's the matter?" he asked.

"I think you do not know what you say, John Slocum. My God! You want a half-breed to be your squaw?"

"No, damn it!" he said angrily. "I want Rosaria's daughter for my wife!"

She looked at him for a moment longer, then flung her arms about his neck and hugged him so tightly he felt his face getting blue. He extricated himself from her grip gently but firmly.

"Is that your answer?" he asked.

She sobered instantly, fear erasing the joy that had blazed a moment before in her face. "Without the gold—there will be no ranch in this high country, and you and I, we will not become man and wife?"

"Oh, hell," Slocum said. "That ain't what I meant. I was just looking for an excuse to ask you to come with me. Forget the gold, if you want."

She smiled brilliantly. "No, we will not forget the gold. Amos told me to take the map. He wanted me to have it. The Apaches can have enough for their rifles, and you and I, we shall have enough for our ranch. Is that not fair enough?"

John grinned. "Sounds fair to me."

She took a deep breath. "Now things will be good. Now we will not just drift. We have a plan. Do you not see, John Slocum? Now we have a reason for doing what we do. It is good. Oh, I love you, John Slocum! And that is the truth of it."

He was humbled by her straightforward, passionate honesty. Reaching over, he pulled her tightly to him and whispered how much he loved her, as well, and for a long while they lay together, until the sun set and they drifted off to sleep once again, still firmly clasped in each other's arms.

Santoro, cradling a gleaming Winchester in his arm, stood erect on a ledge high above the basin, watching impassively as Topaz and John Slocum rode toward the canyon.

The new chieftain of the Moon Dog Lodge of the Mescaleros was bare to the chest, wearing only his buckskin breechclout and the traditional Apache mocassins, the thigh-length, thick-soled footgear that enabled an Apache warrior to cover seventy miles a day on foot. Santoro's thick, lustrous black hair, kept in place by a clean white headband, tugged in the wind as he watched the two riders.

Standing behind Santoro, on a path about six feet below him, a line of silent Apaches awaited the command of their chief. Only two of them carried Winchesters. The rest carried the traditional weapons of the Apache—rawhide slings, elmwood bows in deerskin cases, and the nine-foot-long war lances tipped with steel blades. The bows had a lethal range of a hundred yards, and their slings were capable of hurling stones at least fifty yards farther. Each Apache watched their new chief with eager, impatient eyes, like hounds straining on their leashes.

Santoro watched as the two riders disappeared beyond a huge, humped boulder that shouldered out of the ground. Then he turned and led his war party off the ridge toward their waiting ponies. They moved across the dry ground swiftly, silently, their deerskin moccasins leaving barely a trace.

As Santoro flung himself up onto the back of his pony and led his braves along the ridge, he said nothing to any member of his band. His own thoughts were confused, like a coyote chasing its tail.

When word had come that Topaz and the big white eyes had returned to the mountain stronghold of The People, Santoro felt a deep sadness. He had once wanted Topaz to fill his wickiup with children. But his mother had looked long and hard at the bear claws she flung to the ground and pronounced Topaz an evil woman who would bring nothing but trouble to the Moon Dog Lodge. So he and the other elders of the lodge had done nothing to prevent Topaz from leaving The People when she wished to go in search of her mother's clan.

But then she had returned, and already his mother's

prophecy was coming to pass. With this white eyes, she had slain their chief Naratena in his own wickiup. Later, while fleeing from Santoro, she had called upon the gods to save her, and in response to her magic, the heavens had unleashed a howling torrent, and the gods in her thrall had sent crackling thunderbolts at Santoro and his warriors. Two of his finest braves had been struck black by this woman's terrible power.

Yet still he looked upon Topaz with desire, so much so that even now as he led his braves after her and the white man, his loins trembled with his eagerness to possess her.

Surely this was a terrifying woman.

It was close to dusk. The shadowed mouth of the canyon opened before them. Snaking from it was a small stream, no wider than a foot for the most part.

Slocum glanced at Topaz. "We'll camp inside this next canyon."

She nodded, then looked up at the rocks towering about them. She was looking for Apaches, Slocum knew. The two of them were, in fact, expecting a deputation any time now.

Slocum rode slowly through the narrow defile that led into the canyon. Sheer tawny walls of rock lifted on both sides, almost straight up at times. Well ahead of him, he could see the canyon walls folding away as its floor widened almost into a parkland. In the distance, he detected a line of willows.

"We'll head for those willows," Slocum told her.

Again Topaz simply nodded.

The canyon was a massive, winding slash in the earth that appeared to go on for miles, if what they had already traversed was any indication. For days now they had been riding deeper and still deeper into the Superstition Mountains. This hard, scorched land was in fact a stupendous labyrinth designed by a malevolent god to catch and hold all those unwary or foolish enough to wander into its rocky embrace.

Without Topaz to guide him, Slocum knew he would long since have lost his bearings, like those prospectors and settlers whose skeletons they had seen bleaching in the sun. Slocum had noticed that after a while—and especially under the influence of the maddening sun—all the rocks began to look alike. Exits became entrances, and solid, towering walls appeared where before there had been vistas. And everywhere there was only sand where lush grass to feed a man's horse had been expected.

No one truly knew this land, Topaz had told him, and he believed her. Even Apache war parties might suddenly find themselves disoriented and alone, caught like swarming ants in a sun-blasted, rocky web. And then—as Apache legend had it—when night fell, the ghosts of all those Apache warriors who had died in this place would come out to claim those who had dared to invade their hell.

This explained why this towering, heat-scalded mountain range had been named Superstition Mountains. The Army surveyors and prospectors who had listened to the Apache's tales had given it that name.

As Slocum proceeded down the center of the canyon toward the line of willows, he gazed alertly about him. The smooth walls were broken by strata of umber-colored rock. Great fractures undercut the walls in places, their cavelike interiors hidden in blue shadow, an indication of what this shallow tracery of a stream had once been and might become again whenever the towering peaks about them caught the cloudbursts of the wet season and sluiced great, plunging torrents of water through this canyon.

They came to the willows. They were a feeble, stunted line of trees with a seep just beyond which fed their roots. Dismounting wearily, Slocum decided it would be a better idea to drink from the stream behind them than from the seep. Topaz agreed.

The sun was down by the time they made camp. Jerky, hardtack, and beans, washed down with scalding coffee, was their supper once again. They sat cross-legged before the campfire for a while, both of them too restless to turn in. Slocum had found that Topaz was a superb companion on the trail. Despite her recent wound, she did not complain. She never dropped back. And she was easily as fine a rider as he was.

The thought of the two of them living together in the high country when all this was over warmed his heart. He could not do any better, and he knew it. The trouble was, he wanted it so bad now, he had an unsettling fear that it would never come to pass. Up until now he had never known what it was to have something that good ahead of him. And not having it had given him a freedom of action he no longer felt he had. This, too, had troubled him.

"You are frowning, John Slocum," Topaz said.

She was sitting to one side of him, her luminous eyes studying him carefully. He could not tell her what he felt; it was difficult for him to know precisely himself. So he lied.

"You said the Apaches would find us. Where are they?" he asked.

"We are close enough to their rancheria now. They will come soon, I am sure."

"I am not looking forward to it."

"By now they must have a new chief. I will talk to him. If it is Santoro, I am sure he will listen to what I tell him. And I will show him the scar Naratena left."

"You think that will be enough to excuse the killing of a chief of the Moon Dog Lodge of the Mescaleros?"

She smiled slightly, remembering her own shocked words when Slocum had killed Naratena. "The new chief of the Mescaleros will still want the gold I promised Naratena. And do not forget, only I can read the map."

"I hope it's enough."

"I do, too, John Slocum."

They were silent for a while longer. Then Slocum thought of something else. "Topaz, how did Jacob Waltz manage it? I mean, coming in here regularly to that mine of his with no trouble from the Apaches."

She smiled. "Waltz knew these mountains as well as any Apache, I think. And he was not afraid of the ghosts that prowled these canyons at night."

"How did that help?"

"He would camp sometimes for a week in one spot. The Apaches watching him would grow careless. Then one morning he would be gone."

"Just like that?"

"Yes. The Apaches thought his medicine was very powerful. They thought he was in league with the spirits of the many prospectors who call through these canyons at night."

"How do you explain it, Topaz?"

She looked at him, a tiny glint of humor in her dark, fathomless eyes. "I think maybe the Apaches are right about Jacob Waltz. The spirits of the prospectors, those who howl in the night, must surely help him. I also think Waltz was not afraid of the dark. So that was when he moved. And after that, he moved only at night, hiding like the lizard during the day."

Slocum shook his head. "Hard to believe the Apaches would let him get away like that."

"The Apache is a man like any other. He cannot chase smoke into the sky. He cannot fly like the vulture. Canyon walls will stop him, and so will a bullet. He has no feeling for his enemy. That is what makes him so terrible to the whites. I sometimes think he has no feeling for anyone except his children. But that is no matter."

Again came that enigmatic smile. In the dancing firelight both her eyes and teeth gleamed.

"There is another thing. Whenever Jacob Waltz vanished into these mountains, the Apaches who searched his camp always discovered he had left something for them. Once it was a box of gleaming rifles—repeaters. Another time it was many fine sharp knives, long enough and sharp enough to kill even the grizzly. Once he left many fine blankets, and that winter there was much snow."

Slocum nodded. That sounded more like it. Waltz never took gold from these mountains without leaving a gift behind for The People.

"So now," he said, "you are offering to give the Apaches the gold mine itself."

"Yes. Amos and I made this offer to Naratena

before we returned with the map to find Wall and the others on our trail."

It was pitch dark by this time and the fire had died down. A chill had fallen over the canyon, and the moon had not yet risen above the towering walls enclosing them.

Slocum opened his bedroll. Topaz snuggled in beside him. He folded his arms about her, and she slept almost immediately.

He could not sleep that easily, however. He lay awake, listening to the keening wind cut across the sharp rock faces and its low, mournful howl as it swept through the canyons. It was a chorus of sound that sent shivers up and down his spine, especially when the moon lifted itself finally above the canyon wall and sent its ghastly sheen over everything.

It would be difficult, if not impossible, Slocum realized, for the Apaches not to hear in this shrill, demented chorus the cries of departed souls. And when Slocum went back over what Topaz had told him, he realized he was not entirely certain what Topaz herself believed. At last, his mind still mulling over all that she had told him, Slocum fell asleep.

On a ridge high above the canyon floor, Mat Wall stood up for a moment to gaze down on the sleeping couple. Then he limped painfully back from the rim and sought his own bedroll.

8

Slocum awakened at dawn to the smell of fresh coffee. He opened his eyes and saw Topaz sitting before the fire, examining the map. When she saw him stirring, she refolded the paper and placed it in her bosom. Her eyes shone with excitement.

"We are nearly there," she told him.

He sat up at once, alert and as excited as she. "How far are we?"

"This seep and these willows are in the map. Farther down this canyon, less than a mile, there is a narrow arroyo, very narrow. It leads into a small canyon, and then there is another canyon leading off that one. The mine is in this second canyon. Diablo Canyon it is called on this map."

Slocum grinned and shucked off the slicker. "So let's get something in our bellies and mount up."

She nodded, as pleased as he was. "The coffee is ready now."

They were done with breakfast and Slocum was tightening the cinch on his dun when he heard Topaz utter a tiny, startled cry. He turned quickly, his hand reaching for the Winchester in his saddle scabbard, then froze.

An Apache had stepped from the willows to his right. The squat Indian stood looking at them impassively. Another stepped into view, then another. From the rocks on the far side of the canyon, other Apaches on ponies broke into view and rode toward them. Their chief was in the lead, an erect, handsome Apache with a hooked nose and the piercing eyes of an eagle. His chest was bared and unadorned. He wore only a white headband, breechclout, and Apache moccasins.

"It is as I thought," said Topaz. "Santoro is the new chief."

Well in the lead, Santoro put his pony across the stream and rode to within a few feet of Topaz. Flinging himself from the back of his pony, he spat out what sounded like a curse, then slapped Topaz so hard she reeled away from him, almost collapsing to the ground. His flat, cold face alive with malice, Santoro folded his arms and glared with unabated fury at the stunned Topaz.

With a furious cry, Slocum started for the chief.

But the Apaches on foot swarmed over Slocum before he could take more than a step. He managed to fling one from him, but the other two bore him to the ground.

"No, John!" Topaz cried. "Do not try to fight them!"

But Slocum did not need Topaz to tell him that further struggle was useless as he was flung roughly over onto his face. His hands were jerked behind him and lashed tightly with rawhide.

Slocum twisted his head slightly. "Are you all right, Topaz?"

"Yes," she said. "Do not struggle. I will talk to Santoro."

"I hope so," he muttered as the Apaches binding him turned him roughly over onto his back.

The Apache Slocum had flung to the ground walked over to him and kicked him in the groin. It was a fine shot, placed by an expert, and Slocum closed his eyes and hung on. When he opened them again, Santoro was waiting. The chief bent and struck him across the face, the way a muleskinner would hit a mule, to get his attention.

Slocum could read clearly in the Apache's eyes what he had in mind. And he had no difficulty remembering the fate of Tate Rawson. Things had gone badly for them, Slocum realized glumly. He and Topaz had miscalculated badly.

Topaz came over then and spoke to Santoro in Apache. She spoke rapidly, angrily, and her words stung. Slocum saw Santoro's face wilt before her words. Abruptly, he waved to the other Apaches and Slocum was swept up by strong hands and tied onto his horse.

In a moment the Apaches were ready to move out.

Mounting her horse just ahead of Slocum, Topaz took a quick, concerned glance back at him, then moved out. Santoro was in the lead as the cavalcade of Apaches, riding bareback on their ponies, their flat faces emotionless and still, moved out of the canyon, then turned south.

They left the Superstition Mountains by noon. As they continued south, the heat became a hammer and the ground over which they rode an anvil. The sun hung in a cloudless sky and seemed to have expanded until the entire heavens became a cruel mirror reflecting its fire down upon the baked and gasping land. It was as if the sun were being challenged and was asking that if the rattlesnake, the scorpion, and every other scuttling inhabitant of this land sought shelter from its fierce rays, how then did these creatures on horseback dare to plod arrogantly on across this wasteland of sun and rock?

In such fancies did Slocum lose himself as he crept across this world of pain and heat. With each stride of his pony his swollen, rawhide-bound hands caused him to wince, so intense was the pain. His shirt was soaked through with sweat, his buckskin jacket pressing upon him as heavily as a coat of armor. The salt sweat flowed down his forehead and into his eyes, causing them to sting continuously, as he kept them narrowed against the sun and the withering glare.

Yet within Slocum was not fear for himself as much as fear for Topaz. What would this grim, unforgiving chief do to Topaz once they reached the Apache rancheria? It was grimly amusing now, her belief that it would be possible to reach an agreement with Santoro. And what it showed Slocum was how impossible it was for anyone not a full-blooded Apache to judge properly the depth of savagery these implacable warriors represented.

The distant horizon shimmered in the heat. Sweat poured down Slocum's back. He felt the pain in his hands growing sharper with each passing moment as the rawhide cut deeper and deeper into the raw flesh. He flexed his swollen fingers in an effort to retain some circulation, but the effort only seemed to make matters worse.

But he did not groan or cry out. Instead he watched Topaz as her head slowly bowed before the terrible, unforgiving heat of the sun.

It was close to sundown when they reached the Apache rancheria. As he rode into the village, every eye gleamed at him with studied malevolence. Only the women had smiles, grim, witchlike twists to their wizened faces. Even the younger squaws had this look about them as they peered hungrily at Slocum. He could almost see in their faces what they were thinking.

Here was a white eyes to play with this night, to slice and burn, to pick at and torment. The mescal would bring back the spirits to the rancheria, and their men would lean back on their heels and howl or leap up and dance under the stars, while they would be free to peel back Slocum's skin and peer into his cringing soul. Furthermore, this one appeared strong. He would live long enough for many to count coup on his twisting body!

As Slocum rode through them, some of the squaws crowded close, reaching up to snatch and pinch at him. Some pinched with incredible force, following it up with a high, yipping cry of triumph. Slocum kept himself straight in the saddle, holding his head up, looking neither to the right nor to the left. He was going to die. He knew that by now. But he was not going to die as Tate Rawson had. He would show them that a white man could be as brave as any goddamned Apache.

They pulled up. Slocum was dragged roughly from the saddle. The rawhide was cut from his hands and he was shoved over to a fire. He squatted before it, rubbing his hands briskly together in an effort to soothe the pain.

Santoro walked over and looked down at him. Slocum paid no attention as he continued to massage his hands. They felt better already. Much of the swelling had already gone down. Santoro seated himself and looked across the fire at Slocum.

"You kill Naratena, White Eyes."

"Yes."

"You are brave man to do this."

Slocum made no comment.

"You are also very foolish," Santoro went on.

Slocum continued to massaqe his hands.

"We will see how we will kill you. If your soul is strong, you will give much credit to yourself and to the Apache who kill you."

Slocum looked at the Apache. Could this savage really believe what he was saying? Was that a flicker of a smile he had caught on the chief's impassive face?

Santoro got to his feet and walked away across the camp. Slocum saw Topaz standing with two warriors. It was toward her Santoro was walking. Slocum turned back around and continued to massage his swollen hands. It would not be easy, he realized, to die well, to give credit to the Apache, as the chief had put it. But with Topaz looking on, he must not give way. He could not let her remember him that way.

A squaw left food beside him, and when he had finished it, she brought him a gourd filled with cool water from the spring. He was drinking the last of the water when Santoro returned. A sullen pack of Apaches followed him. Coming to a halt before Slocum, Santoro barked instructions. Two Apaches grabbed Slocum and threw him onto his back. Swiftly, they staked his arms out, leaving his head only inches from the campfire. Santoro spoke again. Another Apache scooped up glowing coals in a piece of bark and dumped them upon Slocum's chest.

He compressed his lips and closed his eyes. The stench of burning hair, then scorched flesh swept into his nostrils. Dimly, through a curtain of pain, he heard Topaz scream. The sound of her running feet came to him. He felt her beside him, bending over him. He opened his eyes and saw her swipe the coals off his chest, then fling herself down upon him, presenting her body as a shield.

She spoke to Santoro in sharp, angry Apache. The man relaxed and stood back, then gave orders to the others. Quick knives sliced through the rawhide holding Slocum to the stakes. Slocum was able to sit up.

"What did you tell him?" he asked.

"I told him I would be his wife. He wants my magic. He thinks it will make him a great chief, greater than all the Apache chiefs, greater even than my father, Emiliano."

"I don't want you to do that," Slocum said.

"It does not matter what you want, John Slocum. In this I decide. But it is not over for you—or for me—yet."

Santoro stepped closer.

"You are not free, White Eyes," Santoro told Slocum. The chief turned and beckoned a glowering Apache closer. "This is Mangas. He is the brother of Naratena. He claims the blood right. It is his privilege."

Slocum flexed the fingers of both hands. A glance at Topaz showed her stepping back, her eyes filled with foreboding. He looked back at Naratena's brother. The Apache was having difficulty holding himself in check. His eyes gleamed like coals.

An old woman who resembled Santoro stepped forward with two knives. After muttering incomprehensible incantations over them, she looked up and nodded to an Apache standing beside her. The Apache quickly traced a large circle with the toe of his moccasin, then stepped back. With surprising dexterity, the old medicine woman flipped a knife into the ground on either side of the circle.

"Do you understand?" Topaz called out to him.

"It looks simple enough," Slocum replied, shucking off his buckskin jacket and shirt and flinging them to one side.

Without warning, Mangas swooped down and plucked the nearest knife from the ground and lunged toward Slocum. Slocum only had time to dodge back as the Apache's blade left a thin tracery across his chest. As Mangas crouched for another lunge, Slocum snatched up the remaining knife and backed up slowly, holding his knife out, blade up, feinting forward repeatedly to keep the Apache offbalance. But soon Mangas ignored Slocum's feints and with a grim smile proceeded to bore relentlessly in on Slocum.

That was what Slocum had been waiting for. He feinted swiftly, but this time he did not pull back. Instead, he slashed all the way forward, aiming for the Apache's right hand. He came closer to the Apache than he expected, however, his blade laying back a long line of flesh on the Apache's chest, the slash extending from his left shoulder all the way down to the right side of his waist.

Ignoring this wound completely, Mangas lunged, slashing back at Slocum. Again he drew blood, this time tracing a long deep slash across Slocum's clavicle. The Apache had aimed for Slocum's jugular, and would have decapitated the white man had his blade reached a couple of inches higher and deeper. It sent a sudden chill through Slocum as Mangas, slashing right and left, drove him steadily back.

The Apache's lightning-like thrusts were almost impossible for Slocum to parry and still think of attacking. Despite his wound, the Apache was enjoying himself hugely, his eyes alight with the triumph that he was certain must come. Crouching low, feinting to the right, then to the left, striking out with the speed of a rattler, he began to slice away at Slocum. Soon Slocum's trousers were in tatters, the hanging pieces heavy with his blood. As Slocum made a desperate lunge in an attempt to catch Mangas off balance, the Apache neatly parried Slocum's knife and then, with a swift counterstroke, opened a fresh wound on Slocum's chest.

It was obvious to Slocum that he could not last much longer. He would soon drop from loss of blood alone. And if he was going to die, he might as well take Mangas with him. He held up, crouching. Mangas did also, his face now cold, his eyes calculating. Slocum waited.

Mangas lunged. Slocum did not try to dodge away. Instead he parried the thrust as well as he could and met Mangas head on, his own blade slicing forward into the Apache. At the same time, he felt Mangas's blade bury itself in the meaty portion of his shoulder. His own blade caught the savage in his left side, then sliced out and free.

Still lunging forward, Slocum's weight drove Mangas to the ground under him. Mangas could not retrieve his blade from Slocum's shoulder, and as he struck the ground under Slocum, Slocum brought his blade up and laid its edge across the Apache's throat, just under his Adam's apple, and pressed. A thin red tongue of the Apache's blood flowed over the gleaming blade.

Slocum looked up at Santoro.

"I could kill him now," Slocum told the chief. "But I already killed his brother. I don't want to kill him, too!"

Santoro looked at Mangas. "This white eyes permits you to live, Mangas. Do you accept?"

Mangas hesitated. Slocum had never looked into eyes filled with such malevolence. It was obvious what Mangas was thinking: If this fool of a white eyes allowed him to live, it would give him the chance to kill the white eyes later.

Mangas grunted his acceptance.

At once, Slocum yanked his knife from the Apache's

throat and pulled himself back, allowing the Apache enough room to withdraw his blade from Slocum's shoulder. It came out easily, a swift freshet of blood following after it. The ground tipped slightly under Slocum, and he found he was having difficulty adjusting his eyes.

And then he sank into the bloody ground.

Slocum was not out for long, and when he regained consciousness he found himself inside a wickiup, Topaz holding his canteen up to his mouth. The water flowed down over his chin as he gulped at it. Never before in his life had anything tasted so good to him.

An old Indian ducked his head into the wickiup and proceeded to rip off the blood-soaked remnants of Slocum's pants. He did not resemble an Apache, and Slocum realized he was probably a Zuni, a tribe noted for its skill in healing. His small, nut-brown face was a spiderweb of wrinkles, his white hair light and feathery.

Reaching into a large, earthen bowl, the Zuni took from it dripping gobs of an evil-smelling poultice and began applying it to the raw, puckered hole in Slocum's chest left by the hot coals, and then to the livid network of knife wounds that covered his arms and legs. The deep knife wound in Slocum's shoulder seemed to give the old Zuni the least trouble, though Slocum found his shoulder was growing stiffer by the minute. When the old man had finished applying the poultices, Topaz helped him to bandage them. This last was accomplished with great speed and deftness. The bandages were not bulky and did not appear to restrict Slocum's movements unduly.

Topaz thanked the Zuni and he left.

"How do you feel, John Slocum?" Topaz asked at last, sitting back on her heels and regarding him.

"I am glad to be alive, if that's what you mean."

"I am glad, too."

"Outside of that, I don't know what else to say. Except maybe we made a mistake coming back for that gold. We'll never see the high country now."

She did not contradict him.

"Did you explain to Santoro what happened—why I had to kill Naratena?" Slocum asked.

"I explained, but it did not help much," she said. "Santoro pointed out that if you had not broken into Naratena's wickiup, you would not have been on hand to kill him."

"The son of a bitch has a point, at that. But did you show him what Naratena did to you?"

"I showed him the scar. He shrugged. Then he said if I had been his woman, he would have cut deeper. He if full Apache, Slocum. There is no Spanish blood in that one."

"And you are going to marry him?" Slocum asked.

"Yes. He has kept his word. He did not let the women have you. I am sorry, John Slocum, but when I saw that coal burning a hole in your chest, I could think only of saving you."

Slocum nodded, too moved by her words to say anything for a moment. Then he spoke again. "Do you think I should have killed Mangas?"

"You must do what you think is best. But to the Apaches, it showed only weakness."

"So now they despise me."

"No. They expect such softness from a white eyes.

You will still have to deal with Mangas. The time will be at his choosing and you will have no warning. You must keep yourself ready at all times."

"Why? I spared his life."

"That is why. Now he must kill you, any way he can. Only then can he free his soul from any obligation to you, here or in the world beyond. As it is now, he has been unable to avenge the death of his brother—and, even worse, his manhood has been tainted by your show of mercy."

"How long am I safe here?"

"As long as it takes for you to heal. Except for Mangas, you no longer have enemies in the Moon Dog Lodge of the Mescaleros," she explained.

"As soon as I am better, I am taking you from here. And the hell with the gold."

"No. I gave my word to Santoro."

"But you don't love him!"

She laughed, a short, bitter bark—and he saw the Apache in her then. "What does this love you speak of matter? He has spared you. I will share his lodge. It must be so."

He felt like a small boy who had just been chastised for asking for the moon. In a sense, she had just told him to grow up; he was in the real world now. He sat back and regarded her, his sense of loss acute.

"Then what about the gold?" he asked.

"I will take Santoro to the mine. Then he will be able to show the other chiefs what fine medicine I bring to the Moon Dog Lodge."

"The other chiefs are causing trouble?"

"He would long since have been chief instead of Naratena, but the chiefs were afraid of his mother.

For a squaw to become the chief Spirit Talker in an Apache lodge is very unusual. Buffalo Woman has already pronounced me a witch, and the other, lesser chiefs know this."

"And if you become Santoro's squaw, they will have two witches to contend with. Is that it?"

She allowed herself a slight smile. "Yes. But it is the gold that will decide the matter—the gold and the many rifles it will bring. There is even some talk of a wagon gun."

"I hope the lesser chiefs say no," said Slocum.

"In that case, Santoro will have to kill me for my part in the death of an Apache chieftain, and your use will be at an end."

"My use?"

"Yes."

"I don't understand."

"The Apache will not dare take by his own hands the wealth that lives in the bowels of the Superstition Mountains. It would be desecration to loot the very body of his gods. The spirits of his ancestors would retaliate with terrible punishment. So others must do this for him." She smiled. "You have been chosen for this task."

Mat Wall had watched with anger and dismay as Slocum and Topaz were taken by the Apaches. Even from his great distance, Wall could sense that Topaz was nearing the mine. As the first light broke over the canyon, he had seen Topaz studying the map. This was the first time he had caught her looking it over. There was no doubt about it. She was close, and she was checking to make sure.

That was when those damned heathen made their move. He had watched the Apaches moving up just before dawn, but there had been nothing he could do about it.

He was close to despair. His wounds had not completely healed, and he was almost certain the bullet in his side was going to have to stay there. His left shoulder was still so painful that he was having to learn all over again how to fire a rifle. Yet, despite all this, he had managed to keep out of the Apaches' way while he tracked Slocum and the girl. And now it looked as sure as Apaches make water in the rocks that his long, long miserable trek into these damned mountains had come to nothing.

Still, it had done his heart good to watch those three Apaches swarm all over Slocum and then slam his face into the dirt; when he saw them binding Slocum's wrists with rawhide he had almost chuckled out loud. Wall knew how deep that rawhide could bite. And that kick in the balls! What a pretty sight that was! It had almost made Wall stand up and cheer.

But, pleasant though that was, Wall guessed he would rather have had the gold. He stood up and trudged back to his horse. The animal was already wilting under the load of extra saddlebags he carried. Mounting up carefully, like an old man, Wall tugged the powerful chestnut around and started back along the ridge. He had gone no more than a quarter of a mile when he pulled up and looked back down at the canyon below.

Damn it! He had come this far already. The Apaches were gone for now. What would be the harm of exploring a little farther on?

Even as this thought occurred to him, he felt a surge of excitement, even hope. Feeling immensely better, he put his horse down the steep slope to his right and headed for the mouth of the canyon through which Slocum and Topaz had ridden the evening before.

Inside the canyon, he stopped at the sink to water his horse and fill his canteens. Then he moved on down the canyon, looking for a sign—any sign at all: wagon tracks, a path, an irregular break in the canyon walls. By noon, he was ready to turn back. The canyon seemed to twist on forever, widening gradually into a stark, brush-covered land that shimmered like a stove top.

He turned about and rode back along the far wall, catching what shade he could from the towering walls. He was about a mile from the willows and was thinking of that seep on the far side of them when he caught sight of something he would have missed had he stayed farther out in the canyon. It was hidden behind a fold in the rock—a towering crevice that appeared to split the canyon wall as high as the eye could see. The crevice was unusual in that it was wide enough to admit a horse and rider, and seemed to extend for a great distance into the rock face. There was something else as well. Though there was grass, stunted and burned brown by the sun, on both sides of the crevice, there was no grass at all at the entrance to the crevice. Not a blade.

Dismounting, Wall inspected the ground. He brushed off the loose sand and placed his hand down flat upon the bare ground. His heart leapt. The ground was solid, rock solid, as if it had been pounded to that consistency by years of hooves.

He turned his horse into the narrow opening and proceeded for at least a hundred yards until the great crack in the rock widened and became a dark, winding arroyo. Following it, he came to another canyon. It was a small, shaded canyon with great overhanging folds of rock blocking out the sun. Wall did not like this place. It was too dark, and he thought he could see the scuttling shadows of scorpions along the walls.

It took him an hour to scour this canyon without much luck. Then he saw, just ahead of him, an arch-way of red rock, and beyond it the walls of still another canyon. As he rode under this archway he glanced up and was startled to see how the rock forming the archway changed in shape until it resembled the head of a scowling devil, horns and all.

Shuddering slightly, Wall kept on until he reached the next canyon. Again he kept his mount close to the walls, looking for any rock formations or clefts that might be hidden from a point farther out, and in less than fifteen minutes he had found the entrance to the Dutchman's mine.

Had he not been looking for it, he would never have found it. A great slab of a rock stood before the entrance, blocking it completely. High over the en-trance, at least fifty feet closer to the canyon rim, hung a massive red boulder. It was sitting on a narrow ledge, suspended by what appeared to be invisible chains. There was no other way to explain why it remained poised as precariously as it did.

Wall dismounted and hurried into the mine. He was so excited he was having difficulty getting his breath. This had to be the Dutchman's mine—and if it were, he would have it all to himself. The Apaches were gone. Slocum would be roast meat by midnight, and God only knew what those Apache devils would do with Topaz.

That left it all to him.

He fairly capered as he darted into the mine's pitch-black entrance. The sudden, paralyzing chorus of fifty or more rattlers filled the air. The sound came from all sides. With a shriek, he turned and raced back out. As he neared the entrance, something struck his boot. He glanced down and saw a rattler hanging to it. Trembling violently with revulsion, he reached down, grabbed the rattler by its tail, and pulled it free, then snapped its neck with a quick flick of his wrist. Still trembling in horror, he flung the snake out into the middle of the canyon.

A quick inspection of his boot revealed that the snake's fangs had not penetrated the leather. At any rate, he had felt nothing. He shook his head in dismay. How could he have been so stupid as to rush in there without first testing for rattlers?

He returned some time after with a smoking brand in one hand, a club in the other, and gently eased himself into the place. The mine entrance was spacious, larger than some living rooms, and all along its cool, hard-packed dirt floor were piles of rattlesnakes, coiling and uncoiling, still disturbed by his previous entrance. And Wall saw something else that was almost as frightening. Scattered here and there over the dirt floor, their bones nearly filled with sand, were the skeletons of others who had tried, like Wall, to steal the Dutchman's gold. Like him, it appeared, they had entered too quickly and the rattlers had caught them. One of them was lying with his arms outstretched, reaching for the mine entrance.

Wall shuddered, then stepped into the entrance and began firing down at the coils of snakes. Those that escaped his rounds began slithering toward the entrance. When all of them were fleeing headlong, he holstered his weapon and began beating at the laggards with the club. Only when Wall was certain there were no more rattlers, in this portion anyway, did he move cautiously on into the mine.

He could not help but admire the Dutchman's industry. The walls and ceilings were shored up with huge, solid timbers, each of them braced so closely that he could not have gotten a knife blade through them. And the place was dry—cool but dry. About twenty feet in, Wall found a storeroom carved out of the rock wall. Inside there was a large, wooden rack containing all the mining tools a man would need: hammers and drills, picks and shovels. Along one wall, tipped up neatly, were two large ore-carrying wheelbarrows. On a table sat four or five kerosene lanterns and beside them a long pine packing crate. Wall opened the lid carefully and saw that it was nearly full of dynamite, the neat sticks sitting in sawdust that was still dry. He pulled out a stick to examine it. Dynamite, he knew, would attract moisture, but there was no water in this mine that Wall could see, and the stick felt dry. He put it back carefully and closed the box.

By this time his torch was smoking and beginning to cut out on him. He set it down, filled one of the lanterns from a bottle of coal oil, and lit it. It took a while for him to adjust the wick, but soon enough he

had a steadier, more reliable light. Raising the lantern
about him, he was more than ever impressed by the
Dutchman's industry. The place was neat, well or-
ganized, and clean. The Dutchman was a one-man
mining operation. Of course the old fox had been
taking gold from this mine for years and had plenty
of time to fix up his place of business. What else did
he have to do with his time?

Thinking back to that nest of rattlers and those
fearsome skeletons guarding the entrance, especially
the poor fellow with his bony arms reaching without
hope for the mine entrance, Wall realized that those
too were a part of the Dutchman's neat arrangements.

But where was the gold?

With mounting excitement, Wall left the storeroom
and moved further into the mine. He was careful not
to move a step along the narrowing shaft without
checking for rattlers first. But since that first mind-
numbing encounter, there had been no more.

At last, after traveling for an indeterminate distance
into the bowels of this mountain, he came upon the
vein. It sat in a wall that reached across the shaft for
at least fifteen feet. Holding up his lantern, Wall saw
the bright gleaming band of precious metal. Gold,
almost pure gold, in a vein at least four feet wide. It
extended from the upper right-hand corner of the shaft
to the lower left-hand corner.

Wall could see some of the blow holes left from
the last series of blasts. He shook his head in admiration. There was no sign of tailings. It even looked
as if the Dutchman had swept the floor clean before
pulling out for the last time. Remembering those neat
wheelbarrows back in the storage room, Wall could

SLOCUM AND THE LOST DUTCHMAN MINE   151

almost see the old geezer trundling load after load out
of the mine to some hidden dump spot.

He sure was a stickler. But that just made it all the
easier.

Wall turned and hurried back through the tunnel
to tend to his horse. He was anxious to set to work.
In his haste, his shoulder lightly brushed a wooden
stick or handle protruding an inch or so from behind
a beam. The piece of wood fell to the floor. Wall
paused. He had not noticed it on the way into the
mine and it was unlike the Dutchman to leave something sticking out like that.

As he bent to pick it up, he felt something strike
his back lightly. And then something else—something that held to his shirt for a moment, then scuttled
off! Wall straightened, his hair standing on end, and
glanced up. An empty wooden box was swinging on
a hinge from a spot between the rafters above him,
and the beams were crawling with tarantulas. Wall
had just emptied a nest of tarantulas upon himself!

Even as he spun back in horror, another one struck
him in the face. In as much terror as Wall, the spider
raced down his face and into his shirtfront. At the
same time, others dropped upon his hat. Two more
landed on his shoulders, while something that felt as
big as his fist was already moving frantically down
his back, caught between his shirt and his skin.

By this time Wall was in full flight. He had dropped
his lantern, and as he ran through the sudden blackness
toward the pinprick of light far ahead of him, he kept
plowing into the beams along the walls or stumbling
over the uneven ground. As he ran, screaming, he
tried to divest himself of his shirt and pants, beating

frantically all the while at the creatures clinging to him.

The first sting was on his thigh, and sent Wall plunging to the ground. A moment later he was bit on the small of his back. Both bites sent numbing shocks coursing through his body. But Wall kept going, his screams sounding strange and smothered in his ears as he flung himself, sobbing with terror, down the long, nightmarish tunnel.

Out in the bright sunlight at last, he leapt upon his horse, his bare back still crawling with three large tarantulas. Roweling his horse fiercely, he rode madly down the canyon, reaching frantically back as he rode in an effort to brush off the tenacious spiders. At last, without sinking their fangs into him, they dropped to the horse's back, then scuttled off.

Wall's knees and both elbows were bleeding. At last, his horse foundering, he pulled up sharply and leapt from his saddle. Dragging his horse up into the rocks after him, he flung himself down onto a clean, unshaded, blistering ledge, and—shivering violently all the while—sat there until sundown, muttering to himself like a madman.

He was still alive by nightfall and was beginning to realize he might survive. As the old prospectors he knew had always insisted, a tarantula's bite was more painful than it was fatal. He wrapped his arms around his knees and stared miserably down at the dark canyon below. He had lost his eye patch somewhere in the mine. With his broken, misshapen face and the dark, puckered hole where his eye should have been, he resembled some pitiful gargoyle just escaped from hell.

And that was precisely how Mat Wall felt.

At last he curled up on the stone and tried to sleep. But he found sleep impossible. He was on fire. The poison quickened and faded within his body, alternately warming, then cooling him. His head ached so that he had disordered visions of it falling off his shoulders and rolling down into the canyon below.

And besides, whenever he closed his eyes, all he could see were the swarming multitudes of scuttling creatures.

9

A week later Slocum found himself part of a column of Apaches reentering the Superstition Mountains. Santoro rode in the lead, with Topaz right behind him. An Apache rode on either side of Slocum, and watchful Apaches kept an eye on him from behind as they led the six packhorses.

Slocum had healed well. The Zuni knew his craft. Aside from a slight ache in his left shoulder, he experienced no difficulty riding. The night before, Topaz had visited Slocum's wickiup and presented him with buckskin leggings and a shirt she had made for him. She had even talked Santoro into allowing Slocum to carry his guns and gunbelt in his bedroll.

Slocum had been glad to see her. Since the day after she had brought the Zuni to doctor his wounds, she had stayed in Santoro's wickiup. She had been installed as the chief's favorite squaw. Slocum made no mention of this to Topaz as he thanked her for her gifts and then discussed the journey before them. She stayed no more than a few minutes, and he was sorry she could not have stayed longer.

As she was leaving, he said he hoped she would be happy as Santoro's squaw. She flung about to stare at him, her eyes fierce, her nostrils flaring. Then she turned quickly and left.

Recalling her reaction, Slocum chided himself. There had been no need for him to have said that. Surely Topaz knew how he felt. Nothing was to be gained by such a remark. Until that moment he had handled everything with commendable reserve— Apache reserve.

He sighed bitterly, his eyes on Topaz as she rode just ahead of him. It was not easy to think of her with that savage. He wondered if Topaz had any more wounds. Or had she learned to be obedient? For the first time Slocum realized why some men killed over a woman.

And it did not help him to know that Topaz had consented to be Santoro's squaw in order to save Slocum's life.

The entrance to the canyon loomed. They rode on through. Once they were in the canyon, Slocum saw

Topaz boot her pony up beside Santoro. They rode on past the willows for about a mile; then Topaz pointed out to Santoro a great fold of rock jutting out from the canyon wall off to their right. The column headed for it. Once they had skirted it, they found themselves riding toward a deep but very narrow crevice in the rock wall.

They went on through in single file, came out into a darker canyon, and headed toward another canyon running off this second one. To reach it they had to ride under a natural stone archway of red sandstone. Slocum glanced up as he passed under it and saw the bulging rock slowly transform itself into the head of a devil. At once Slocum remembered Topaz telling him that the canyon they were looking for was called Diablo Canyon.

Once they were inside Diablo Canyon, Topaz guided them without hesitation to the Dutchman's mine. There was an enormous boulder sitting before it, partially concealing the mine entrance from view. As they pulled up before it, Slocum saw Santoro and Topaz dismount and almost immediately begin to examine the ground in front of it. There was more discussion, in which other Apaches hurried forward to join, and it was not long before two of the Apaches mounted up and moved off down the canyon. As they rode, they studied the ground before them.

Slocum dismounted and headed for the mine entrance. Topaz left Santoro to meet him halfway.

"What's up?" Slocum asked her.

"Someone has been here recently."

"How recently?"

"Santoro says a week ago."

Most of the Apaches were standing well back of the entrance, their faces reflecting the awe with which they viewed their present mission. They were in the accursed Land of the Wailing Spirits, and soon they would be asked to carry away the treasure these spirits had stored deep in their bowels. It was a grim, frightening prospect; but the Apaches did their best to hide their terror.

"And no further tracks since then?" Slocum asked, glancing up at the walls towering over them.

"No."

"Strange."

"No, not so strange," Topaz said.

"What do you mean?"

"Amos Blucher said the Dutchman warned him when he gave him the map to watch out for his surprises."

"Surprises? What kind of surprises?"

"Amos thought he meant the hidden traps the Dutchman always placed in the mine to catch any who entered to steal his gold."

"What were some of these traps?"

"Nests of rattlesnakes, scorpions, and tarantulas, Amos said. Gila monsters, too, whenever he could find any."

"You think whoever made those tracks might be dead now?"

Topaz shrugged. "The tracks showed someone entering, then running out and mounting up very fast. There is no telling how far he got. But from the look of those tracks, he was in a great hurry."

"I think I know who might have made those tracks," Slocum said.

Topaz nodded grimly. "Mat Wall."

"If he's still around here, he'll soon wish he'd gone someplace else. Those two Apaches Santoro sent after him looked pretty efficient."

Topaz nodded. "Are you ready?"

"I suppose so."

"I'll tell Santoro. He is very nervous this deep in the mountains, and he did not like that devil we passed."

"Did he say anything?"

She smiled coldly. "No, but he muttered something."

Mat Wall had almost given up. Then he had seen the dust trail and, not long after, the file of Apaches riding through the narrow arroyo into the smaller, darker canyon. He kept to the ridges and was peering directly down upon them when they passed under the limestone arch and pulled up finally in front of the mine entrance.

When he saw the two mounted Apaches move off down the canyon, he knew they were following his trail, but it did not bother him unduly. Once he had gained the rocks, he had covered his trail well enough to prevent his being followed, even by an Apache. And his chestnut was well hidden. But from now on, he would have to be careful, very careful. The Apaches would be looking for him—and so would Slocum.

That the Apaches had let Slocum live surprised Wall. The man must have reached some deal with the savages. But what had really surprised Wall was the sight of Topaz and the Apache chief riding together at the head of the column, with Slocum well back and apparently under guard.

Well, that was just fine with Mat Wall. He would

sit back and wait and, when the time came, he would deal himself in. He would let Slocum and those damned Apaches take their own chances in that hellish netherworld. For his part, he would sure as hell never enter that mine again. Even recalling for a moment what he had been through was enough to make him quake inwardly. Enough was enough.

Still peering down, he saw Slocum cautiously entering the mine. Shuddering in vicarious horror at what that big son of a bitch would soon be facing, Wall pulled back from the rim and returned to his shelter in the cliff face. It was a small cavern, its floor and sides smooth. Buffed by centuries of wind-laden sand, it had become a cubicle that held not a hidden corner nor a single crevice. Here Mat Wall was safe from the scuttling creatures that still populated his nightmares.

Pulling his knees up to his face, he stared with his one red-rimmed eye at the towering rock wall across the canyon from him. Hatless, his pants in tatters, his upper torso scorched black from the sun, he was as much a part of the canyon's wildlife now as any scorpion or tarantula.

But this realization had not yet occurred to him.

Slocum had thrown a rock into the mine entrance and had heard at once the commotion that had erupted. The massive number of agitated rattlers gave off a sound akin to a single high-pitched scream. Peering in cautiously, he glimpsed first the warning skeletons the Dutchman had placed neatly about. Then, as his eyes grew accustomed to the gloom, he saw the ground undulating with rattlesnakes. It looked as if the Dutchman had flung an enormous can of giant night crawlers into the place.

He went back for a torch and told Santoro what he wanted. The chief listened impassively, then gave orders. At once the Apaches searched out dry wood and branches to use as clubs and moved unhappily toward the mine entrance. Slocum tucked his pants well down into his boots and stepped cautiously into the mine, his club in one hand, the torch held high in the other. The flaring, guttering flame caused the disturbed snakes to draw swiftly into a coil, the shriek of their combined rattles almost deafening Slocum. But the moment he began clubbing the snakes within reach, the rest turned tail and began corkscrewing from the place. Outside, the Apaches took care of the fleeing reptiles. Slocum could hear their cries and the sound their clubs made as they pounded the ground about them.

Moving further into the mine then, Slocum killed one more rattler by picking it up and snapping its neck. After that he saw no more. But this did not make him feel any easier. Moving cautiously on up the mine shaft, his torch held out in front of him for protection as well as for light, he caught sight of an empty wooden box hanging down from a roof beam. Peering up at it, he saw two, then three large, hairy spiders scurrying into the shadows of the beam. Tarantulas. This box had been their nest, apparently. That would account for Mat Wall's hurried exit—if the intruder had indeed been Mat Wall.

He ducked quickly past the spot and soon came to the storeroom. He was pleased at what he saw, especially the dynamite. When he finally reached the end of the mine shaft and saw the tremendous vein of almost pure gold he pulled up in astonishment and uttered a long, low whistle. That crazy Dutchman really had something, after all. His own King Solomon's mine.

And now it belonged to the Apaches.

Slocum returned to Santoro and told him what he would need. He fully expected the chief to protest, and in that he was not disappointed. Santoro shook his head emphatically.

Topaz hurried over. "What is wrong?" she asked Slocum.

"I want the Apaches to help. I'll have to blast the gold from the rock, and I can't manage that without their help."

Topaz turned to Santoro and explained. Again, Santoro refused. The two had a short, sharp exchange. Then Topaz turned back to Slocum.

"He says no Apache will enter the sacred mountain of his people. Only the White Eyes can do such a thing. For you, he says, this will be no crime. These are not your spirits that dwell here."

"And it's not my gold I'm digging. Tell him if I don't get the help I need, I won't be able to get the gold."

"You lie, White Eyes!" Santoro said, deciding in his anger to address Slocum directly.

Slocum met the Apache's stare boldly. "Now you listen to me, Santoro. If I have to blast that gold out by myself, it is going to take a long time. You and your Apaches will be camping here for many days."

"How many?"

"A week, two weeks."

This answer obviously dismayed Santoro. He did not like this place any more than his braves did. The prospect of camping in this land of wailing shadows for such a long time was not something he relished.

Topaz spoke up then, addressing Santoro in Apache. The conversation was brief. Slocum could see the chief denying her proposal the first time, then reluctantly, angrily, giving in as she persisted.

Topaz turned to Slocum. "I am only half Apache," she said, a gleam of triumph in her eyes. "So I will be able to join you inside the mine. I will help you."

"Damn it, that place is dangerous, Topaz. I don't know what else that crazy Dutchman has in store for us. Looks to me like he already emptied a nest of tarantulas down onto Mat Wall."

Santoro spoke up. "Topaz will help you, White Eyes. See that she does not come to harm."

Slocum did not bother to reply to the chief. Turning to Topaz, he said, "All right, then. Keep behind me and watch your step."

While Topaz held the drill, Slocum drove it into the speckled vein with powerful, measured blows of his sledgehammer. Topaz had caught on quickly. She did not flinch away, and after each blow she turned the drill just enough, then held it steady for Slocum's next stroke. As he swung the sledgehammer, Slocum perspired freely. He did not want to miss the drill and strike Topaz's hand.

They had already drilled three blow holes, and were starting on what Slocum hoped would be the last one before they blasted. Stepping back to mop his brow, Slocum noticed movement out of the corner of his eye. He turned quickly and saw a number of scorpions dropping to the floor from a beam and scurrying off into the darkness. He lowered his hammer and pulled back to look more closely at the wall from which the scorpions had come. Three lanterns burning coal oil sent a steady but feeble light at the rock face they were drilling and at the solid timbers holding up the sides and bracing the overhead beams.

"What's the matter?" asked Topaz.

"I don't think that Dutchman is finished with us yet."

As he spoke, he took down one of the lanterns and walked over to the beam. Cut into the wall alongside it he saw a long, narrow chamber. He held the lantern up to the chamber and peered in. Slocum glimpsed small, scurrying insects, each one of which had a hooked tail quivering over its back. Scorpions! Swarms of them! Thousands, perhaps millions! Slocum shuddered involuntarily and felt the hair stand up on the back of his neck. A tarantula's bite was painful but seldom fatal. But two or three scorpions on a man could kill him. And his death would not be quick or easy.

Swiftly, Slocum circled the chamber. There were similar apertures on each wall except the rock face. And inside each chamber were more swarms of similarly agitated scorpions. Now that he was alerted to the danger, he glanced down and saw a number of scorpions scuttling about along the dirt floor, keeping close to the walls.

Topaz followed his gaze and gasped softly.

"I think we'd better get out of here for now," he said.

She nodded quickly. Slocum backed up swiftly, moving back down the mine shaft toward the supply room. As he did so, he scanned the walls and ceilings much more closely than he had earlier.

This time he did not miss it. As he moved past a sharp bend in the shaft, he looked up and found a wrought-iron gate recessed cleverly into the ceiling about ten paces beyond the bend. The gate was wide enough to close off the entire passage. Using his lantern and searching patiently, Slocum saw that the gate was hinged in such a manner as to swing down and lock into place, its steel-tipped footings digging securely into the dirt floor.

But what was needed to trigger the gate and release the scorpions?

He moved cautiously back around the sharp bend in the shaft and stared thoughtfully at the rock face. Its single broad stripe of gold gleamed in the light of the two remaining lanterns and Slocum could make out the three blow holes they had already drilled.

In that instant it came to him. Dynamite was the trigger!

Anyone blasting into that vein would be huddled behind this bend in the shaft, waiting for the debris to settle. The explosion would arouse the scorpions to a frenzy and at the same time release the gate. As it slammed into place, trapping the gold-seeker between it and the rock face, the insects would swarm out of their chambers and stream down the mine shaft. The hapless intruder would find himself clawing at the gate, trapped. He would die, screaming, under a tide of enraged scorpions. It was clear now where Jacob Waltz had obtained those skeletons he had left on display just inside the mine entrance.

"I think we should go back to the supply room for dynamite," he told Topaz.

She did not question him, but as they returned to the room he explained to her what he had in mind. Leaving the mine, he retrieved a couple of cigars from his bedroll, and also his tin of sulphur matches. Lighting one of the cigars as he passed a lounging Apache, he exhaled luxuriously. Inside the supply room, he lifted a coil of fuse out of the box of dynamite, and cut off a six-inch section. He lit it by touching the glowing end of his cigar to it.

The end sputtered to life, the fuse curling as the fire crept through the powder that filled it. He timed it mentally to see how long it took to burn through six inches of this particular fuse. Satisfied that the fuses could be trusted, he took out three sticks of dynamite from the box and bound them together with strands of wire he cut from a coil he found in a corner. Using his knife to hollow out one end of a dynamite stick, he inserted the cap and a foot of the fuse, tamping it in securely with some of the soft explosive.

He made one other makeshift bomb, this one with a shorter fuse, and placed them carefully down on the table. There was a barrel of coal oil sitting on a frame in the far corner. He filled a jug with the oil, returned to the rock face, and poured it liberally over the dirt floor. It took six jugs of coal oil to saturate the dirt floor to his satisfaction.

"Keep well behind me," he told Topaz as he put down the jug and picked up one of his bombs. He handed her the other one, explaining to her when he would need it.

"And don't follow me beyond that gate," he warned her as they started back up the mine shaft.

A moment later, a few yards beyond the bend in the shaft, Slocum touched his cigar to the fuse, then tossed the bomb toward the rock face. He held his breath as it struck the ground. It did not go off. He watched it a second longer as it rolled all the way, bumping to a halt finally against the rock face, its sputtering fuse still alive. Turning, he bolted back toward the bend in the mine shaft and called to Topaz.

She tossed him the second bomb, the one with the shorter fuse. He caught it, lit the fuse, and threw it just a short distance along the tunnel. Ducking back around the bend, he pulled up beside Topaz on the other side of the gate. The first bomb detonated. Almost immediately afterward, another, closer detonation rocked them as the second bomb exploded. The ground under their feet shuddered and from the walls and the ceiling above them sifted sand and debris.

But no scorpions.

Meanwhile, right on schedule—the powerful detonations obviously triggering some mechanism in the ceiling—the gate swung down and buried its sharp footings into the floor of the mine shaft. Behind the gate, tongues of fire swept toward them along the oil-saturated dirt floor. Great black, billowing clouds of smoke enclosed the iron gate, while sheets of flame whipped at them, pushing them back.

They fled down the mine shaft and out into the bright day.

Slumping wearily down onto the ground a safe distance from the mine, Slocum puffed on his cigar and let Topaz advise Santoro that he and his braves had better stay clear of the mine entrance until the few scorpions which managed to get through that blazing coal oil made good their escape.

The next day Slocum went back into the mine and dug around the gate's footings, loosening them enough to rip it free of the track and hinge the Dutchman had fashioned in the sides of the timbers. Not until the gate had slammed down did the tracks become invisible. It was as if the Dutchman was in league with the Devil, so diabolically clever was the device.

By the end of that day Slocum was able to begin blasting. He worked almost through the night, sleeping for only a few hours, and by noon the next day, Santoro and his braves were ready to pull out, their packhorses' aparejos bulging with almost pure nuggets of gold.

By that time, Slocum was close to exhaustion. He and Topaz had been using the heavy wheelbarrows to transport the gold ore from the mine. His only respite had been seeing the Apaches finally working. As he and Topaz dumped the gold ore, tailings and all, in front of the mine entrance, the impatient Santoro, anxious to leave the mountains by sundown, directed his men to take the gold from there and pack the aparejos. Never in his life had Slocum seen grown men who had such an aversion to hard work. It was a sight to warm his heart to watch these unhappy savages bending and carrying.

There was no more gold to trundle and Slocum was returning the biggest wheelbarrow to the supply room when Topaz caught up with him. Her face was white, her eyes blazing in cold fury.

"What is it, Topaz?" he asked.

"You were to be allowed to go free. Is that not so?"

"That's right," Slocum said, immediately alert. He patted his two bulging saddlebags. "I'll be on my way as soon as you and Santoro pull out. I figure there's enough here to set me up for a good long while. I picked each one of these nuggets with great care."

"Santoro has changed his mind."

Slocum was not surprised. He almost laughed out loud. "Why, that can't be, Topaz. An Indian never changes his mind, never goes back on his word. It just ain't done. It's the white eyes, those with the forked tongues, who go back on their word."

"You believe that, do you?" she asked.

"Nope, and I don't believe in fairies, neither."

"Well, Santoro believes in spirits. And he is convinced he and his people will be cursed if they let those who broke in and looted this mountain go free. By not letting you escape punishment for this, the Moon Dog Lodge of the Mescaleros will escape the curse of the spirits that dwell in these mountains."

"On what authority does he have that, Topaz? That old crone, his mother?"

Topaz nodded. "It is possible. Before Santoro left, she might have advised him."

"Ain't he planning to use this here tainted gold to buy rifles and wagon guns?"

"Yes."

"Then what's he going to do when he runs out?"

"When Santoro wants more gold, he will capture other whites and use them as he has used you."

"Makes a kind of sense at that," Slocum commented sardonically. "Well, don't you worry, Topaz. I won't be going quietly. Fact is, I wasn't going quiet, anyway."

"What do you mean?"

"That's my secret, Topaz. You go on back to your chief now, but keep your pretty head down."

"Slocum, there is something else I must tell you."

There was a bitter tone to her voice that alerted him. He looked at her more closely. "I'm listening, Topaz."

"I have been helping you."

"So?"

"I am as guilty as you are. I, too, have been digging at the roots of this mountain. I, too, have been taking its wealth."

"Now, wait just a minute there, Topaz. You don't mean Santoro is going to..."

"No, Santoro will not kill me. But I am no longer his woman. I have been given to the old Zuni. And before the old man will be allowed to take me as his squaw, I am to be properly scourged so that I will remain an object of scorn, a warning to all who would do as I have done."

"Scourged?"

"I will be whipped. Scars will be left on my body and my face."

"No, they won't, Topaz. You're coming with me."

She shook her head. "You talk bravely, but you have no weapons. And Santoro and the others await you just outside the mine entrance. You are trapped."

"But you came to warn me."

"Yes."

"Does Santoro know that?"

"He saw me run in here. Yes."

"Then don't be so sure he will not kill you."

She flung her head back and spoke with quiet defiance. "I would rather die at your side than live at his, or with any other Apache. He knows that now."

Slocum pulled Topaz close. Instead of kissing her on the lips, he stroked her hair and drank in the fragrance of her. She had worked very hard beside him these past two days, and once again it had reminded him of what a fine partner she would make. Maybe, just maybe, they might make it to that high country together, after all.

Slocum turned back to the table, slung his saddlebags over his shoulder, then tucked the bundle of dynamite he had already fashioned down into his shirt. From what Topaz had just told him, he was going to have to use it a little bit sooner than he had expected. He thought a minute, snatched one more stick of dynamite out of the sawdust, swiftly fashioned a short fuse for it, then stuck it into his belt.

"Ready?" he asked, taking a fresh cigar from his pocket and clipping off its end with a pocket knife.

Topaz nodded.

Slocum thumbed a lucifer to life and held it to the end of his cigar. "Stay right behind me, Topaz. And keep yourself loose. Hear?"

"Yes, John Slocum, I hear."

Slocum's cigar glowing in the dark tunnel, he and Topaz started down the mine shaft toward the bright rectangular patch of sunlight.

10

When Slocum reached the mine entrance, he peered out and saw the Apaches waiting patiently. All of them were mounted up by this time, and each brave was facing the mine entrance. Santoro and two of his lieutenants were holding their Winchesters; the rest had their bows out.

Topaz, standing close beside Slocum, peered out also.

He glanced at her. "Ask the son of a bitch what he has in mind. If he's going to let you out of here, you could maybe get my horse ready."

She cleared her throat and called out to Santoro. In Apache, she asked him why he and his braves were waiting so grimly for Slocum and her to emerge from the mine. His answer was short and blunt, and sounded to Slocum like the bark of a vicious dog.

Topaz pulled back and looked at Slocum. "He no longer considers me Apache. I am white. We will be slain together and left to appease the spirits of these mountains."

"All right. Now listen carefully. We are going to have to move very fast in the next few minutes. Over there—and there," Slocum told her, using his cigar to point out two caches he had stashed near the entrance, "are very powerful bombs I built last night. When they go off, they will more than likely seal this mine. I had planned to set them off after you and Santoro left. But he has forced my hand, looks like, and I am going to set them off now, as a diversion."

"But we'll be killed!"

"I don't think so. When I give the word, make a dash to that boulder outside. Once you are safe, I'll light the fuses and follow you. When the mine blows, there will be enough confusion for us to make our way down the canyon. It's not much, but it's the only chance we've got."

She nodded quickly and moved closer to the entrance. Peering out into the blazing sunlight, she gathered herself to run. A rifle shot came from one of the Apaches alongside Santoro, the bullet whining off a beam inches above Topaz's head.

She pulled back and looked at Slocum.

"Hold it," he said. "Hold it. You're right. It doesn't

look like we're going to get very far that way. Either of us."

Topaz shivered slightly. That round had come very close.

"Move aside," Slocum said softly.

He pulled out the single stick of dynamite he had thrust into his belt, touched his cigar to the fuse, then flipped the dynamite out of the mine toward the waiting Apaches. Poking his head out to watch, he saw the Apaches peer for a moment at the tumbling stick, then pull back in panic as they realized what it was.

As Slocum watched in dismay, the fuse sputtered out, and the dynamite came to rest harmlessly against a rock. The Apaches wheeled their mounts and rode swiftly back up to the mine entrance, their faces showing their contempt. They were no longer afraid of Slocum's dynamite.

"That's fine," Slocum said with grim triumph. "Just ride right on up to the mine, you bastards, and get what's coming to you." As he spoke, he took from his shirt one of the larger bombs he had fashioned earlier.

He lit the fuse and flung the bomb out of the mine. It struck the boulder in front of the entrance and glanced off, soaring over the heads of the Apaches. It landed just behind them, and Slocum caught a glimpse of it rolling to a halt and saw the fuse sputtering. He waited while the Apaches, no longer so sure of themselves, began to mill about nervously.

The fuse sputtered out and the bomb sat there. The Apaches howled with derision and turned back again to the mine entrance. For the first time Slocum felt despair. There was still half a box of dynamite back there, but it was the fuses that were giving him trouble. They had been doing so all during the blasting, but he had been patient. He could no longer afford to be so patient. What fuse he had left was evidently the most deteriorated part of the coil.

Slocum peered out at Santoro. What passed for a smile was on the chief's flat face. He was about to ask for a chance to palaver when a rifle shot rang out from the rocks above. An Apache behind Santoro pitched forward from his pony. Another rifle shot sounded, then another. The Apaches were caught in a merciless enfilade as the rifleman above them poured fire down upon their close ranks. Two more Apaches were knocked from their ponies, while Santoro and those with rifles lifted them and began firing back at whoever it was above them.

"Mat Wall!" cried Slocum. "It must be him!"

As he spoke, he hurried over to the bomb caches and lit each fuse. These were early, drier fuses. He watched them burn for a moment, noting the bright sparkle as the flame raced along the fuse. Satisfied, he hurried back to Topaz. There was no going back now.

"Keep behind me," he told her.

He darted from the mine. The Apaches were in disarray, wheeling their horses in confusion, some firing frantically up at the rifleman, others unleashing futile arrows. In the confusion, not a single shot was fired at Topaz and Slocum as they darted from the mine and raced over behind the towering boulder that guarded the mine entrance.

Slocum glanced up at the dim figure outlined against the bright sky. Yes, it was Mat Wall. There was no way he could mistake that broken face.

Then, without warning, Wall began firing down at them.

As the bullets whined off the rocks about them, Slocum darted for cover. That was when the two bomb caches inside the mine detonated. The explosions were almost simultaneous. So powerful were they that the canyon wall seemed to lift off the canyon floor. A rush of stone and earth exploded out the mine entrance, resembling grapeshot from a cannon.

The nearest Apaches were knocked from their ponies, while the ponies themselves staggered under the impact. Slocum did his best to protect Topaz by shielding her with his body, but in a second he too was covered with debris. A stone the size of his fist missed his skull by inches and careened off.

"Look!" Topaz cried, pointing up.

Slocum followed her gaze and saw a great boulder poised on a narrow ledge high above the mine entrance. It appeared to be no longer stable. Rocks and clods of earth began to fall away from its base. At that moment a large patch of the canyon wall about ten yards below it simply gave way. At once, the boulder tipped forward and began to roll ponderously down the steep slope. It bounded once, twice, then settled into a steady, terrifying plunge that brought with it trees, brush, smaller boulders, shale, and sand. The canyon shook with the roar of its descent. Slocum pulled Topaz away from the boulder and both of them ran as far as they could up the canyon away from the mine entrance. They were none too soon, as the slide buried the mine entrance under tons of rock and dirt.

The boulder, however, seemed to have a life of its

own. Preceded by a swarm of smaller boulders, it shot across the canyon in a cloud of debris, overtaking three fleeing Apaches and obliterating them, ponies and all. Thundering on across the canyon floor, it smashed into the wall opposite and, with a titanic crunch, disintegrated into great, jagged chunks.

The silence that followed was awesome—almost as frightening as the ear-splitting cataclysm that had preceded it.

The Apaches were gone. Those who had not been shot down by Wall or smote by the thundering hand of the avalanche had turned their ponies and ridden off in disarray, even leaving behind two of the gold-laden packhorses. The terrible, vengeful spirits of this place had spoken to them with a shattering finality. They did not have to be told twice.

"I don't see Wall," Topaz said, peering up at the rim.

He followed her gaze. "I don't think you will again," he said, after a moment. "The ridge he was standing on has disappeared. It went with the rest of the wall, looks like."

"He saved our lives."

"He did. But his intent was to get that gold. He could not have been thinking very clearly, though. There were too many Apaches for him. He could not have killed them all, and they would have tracked him and killed him long before he left these mountains."

They walked back to what had been the entrance to the Dutchman's mine. He had planted those two bombs originally because he had wanted simply to seal off the entrance so that the Apaches would not be able to use this mine as their own private treasury.

He had succeeded, however, in doing much more than that. The entire face of the canyon had shifted and collapsed inward, like an old man's cheek. The boulder which had served as a sentinel outside the entrance was entirely covered. There was now no way anyone could tell that a mine had once been tunneled out of that canyon wall. Soon, Slocum knew, the cloudbursts of the rainy season would sweep away the loose sand and debris, bunch grass would take hold, the talus would build up, and in years to come this Dutchman's mine would become only a wild, improbable tale told by old men around campfires at night.

It took a while for Slocum to dig his saddle and bedroll out of the debris that blanketed the campsite on the far side of the canyon. After a search that took him past two dead Apaches and a third who was dying with one of Mat Wall's bullets in his lung, Slocum found his dun running with a nervous remuda of Apache ponies well down the canyon.

Early the next morning, trailing the two packhorses the Apaches had left, Slocum and Topaz set out, heading north. Two days later, almost out of the Superstition Mountains, they were climbing a steep trail when Slocum glanced at Topaz. He was frowning.

"Someone's trailing us," he told her.

She glanced quickly back, then looked at him. "You have seen him?"

"There's been occasional dust, that's all."

"Do you want to stop and go back?"

"No. Keep going. We'll be out of these mountains by nightfall. Just keep your eyes open."

They pulled up onto the crest of the ridge and rode along it for a while, Slocum glancing back every now and then. The dust on their backtrail was gone. Indeed, he had seen nothing for more than an hour. Perhaps it had only been his imagination—or a dust devil.

But Slocum did not believe that explanation, and a second later, as they rode side by side through a narrow defile, he heard Topaz gasp. He turned to her just as she flung herself from her saddle onto him, knocking him violently sideways. As he tumbled off his horse, a small, dark Apache arrow blossomed in her back.

He struck the hard ground. His senses reeling, he heard the packhorses bolt back down the trail. Topaz collapsed onto him, the arrow protruding from her back. Slocum scrambled to his feet. An Apache dropped to the trail about ten yards ahead of him and crouched, waiting.

It was Mangas.

The Apache flung his elmwood bow aside and straightened. Pulling his knife from its sheath, he said, "Now we fight once more. You will have my soul no longer. This time I will cut out your heart!"

He pulled another knife from his rawhide sling and tossed it to the ground in front of Slocum. Then he flung his sling aside and started forward. Slocum drew his .44, aimed quickly, and fired. The bullet stamped a neat hole in the Apache's bronzed chest. It staggered him. Slocum fired again . . . and again . . . and again . . . .

It was night. Since the ambush, they had not traveled far, and were still caught in the brooding embrace of the Superstition Mountains. Topaz was not doing well. Slocum had pulled the shaft from her back, but he had been unable to control entirely the flow of blood that surged out after it. She had become too weak to ride not long after; now, as he built the fire up some and glanced over at her, he realized she was not going to make it this time.

Naratena's knife wound had taken all her reserves. She had nothing left.

"I'm thirsty," she said.

He brought over her canteen. Lifting her head onto his lap, he placed its neck into her mouth and tipped it up carefully. She drank raggedly, spilling most of the water down her chin. Her eyes appeared to be on fire, but her face was as pale as the moonlight bathing it.

She pushed the canteen feebly away and smiled up at him. "We aren't going to make it to the high country together, are we?"

"No," he said, "I guess not."

"Too bad. We work well together. By day—and in the night, too." A trace of her old passion flashed up at him.

Slocum tried to swallow, but it was like someone had him by the throat. His vision blurred and he looked quickly away.

"John Slocum, there is a locket in my bedroll. It is the one my mother gave me. I want you to have it. Keep it and remember me. For a while, I was your betrothed, is that not so?"

"Of course," Slocum managed.

"One kiss," she said with sudden urgency. "Now!"

He bent quickly and closed his lips over hers. They

responded for only an instant, then grew slack. He sat back up, looked for a moment down into her vacant eyes, then rocked back on his heels like an Indian as the tears streamed down his face.

He left her high in the rocks, tucked into a hidden ledge, as close as he could manage to the way she had left old Amos Blucher. Then he mounted up. He had no heart left in him for what it would take to chase back into the mountains for those two pack-horses; and as he sat his horse, he emptied the gold nuggets out of his saddlebags and watched them bounce erratically over the ridge and out of sight.

He had entered this cruel land in search of a murderer with nothing but the few coins in his bag. The Apaches had found his murderer for him, and for a short while he had experienced a love that had warmed him and shaken him. He had not realized it was possible for him to feel that strongly, to want someone so much. Now all that was behind him. Topaz was gone, and he would leave the Superstition Mountains the way he had entered them. Alone and near broke.

He clapped his spurs to his dun and continued north, to a cooler, more kindly land, he hoped.

JAKE LOGAN

J.D. HARDIN

"THE MOST EXCITING WESTERN WRITER SINCE LOUIS L'AMOUR"
—JAKE LOGAN

____	872-16840-9	BLOOD, SWEAT AND GOLD	$1.95
____	872-16842-5	BLOODY SANDS	$1.95
____	872-16882-4	BULLETS, BUZZARDS, BOXES OF PINE	$1.95
____	872-16877-8	COLDHEARTED LADY	$1.95
____	867-21101-6	DEATH FLOTILLA	$1.95
____	872-16844-1	THE GOOD THE BAD AND THE DEADLY	$1.95
____	867-21002-8	GUNFIRE AT SPANISH ROCK	$1.95
____	872-16799-2	HARD CHAINS, SOFT WOMEN	$1.95
____	872-16881-6	THE MAN WHO BIT SNAKES	$1.95
____	872-16861-1	RAIDER'S GOLD	$1.95
____	872-16767-4	RAIDER'S REVENGE	$1.95
____	872-16839-5	SILVER TOMBSTONES	$1.95
____	867-21133-4	SNAKE RIVER RESCUE	$1.95
____	867-21039-7	SONS AND SINNERS	$1.95
____	872-16869-7	THE SPIRIT AND THE FLESH	$1.95
____	867-21226-8	BOBBIES, BAUBLES AND BLOOD	$2.25
____	06572-3	DEATH LODE	$2.25
____	06138-8	HELLFIRE HIDEAWAY	$2.25
____	867-21178-4	THE LONE STAR MASSACRE	$2.25
____	872-16555-8	THE SLICK AND THE DEAD	$1.50
____	06380-1	THE FIREBRANDS	$2.25
____	06410-7	DOWNRIVER TO HELL	$2.25
____	06152-3	APACHE GOLD	$2.25
____	06001-2	BIBLES, BULLETS AND BRIDES	$2.25
____	06331-3	BLOODY TIME IN BLACKWATER	$2.25
____	06248-1	HANGMAN'S NOOSE	$2.25
____	06337-2	THE MAN WITH NO FACE	$2.25
____	06151-5	SASKATCHEWAN RISING	$2.25
____	06412-3	BOUNTY HUNTER	$2.50
____	06743-2	QUEENS OVER DEUCES	$2.50

Available at your local bookstore or return this form to:

BERKLEY
Book Mailing Service
P.O. Box 690, Rockville Centre, NY 11571

Please send me the titles checked above. I enclose _____. Include 75¢ for postage and handling if one book is ordered; 25¢ per book for two or more not to exceed $1.75. California, Illinois, New York and Tennessee residents please add sales tax.

NAME _____

ADDRESS _____

CITY _____ STATE/ZIP _____

(allow six weeks for delivery.)

LONGARM

Explore the exciting Old West with
one of the men who made it wild!

___07524-8	LONGARM #1	$2.50
___06807-1	LONGARM ON THE BORDER #2	$2.25
___06809-8	LONGARM AND THE WENDIGO #4	$2.25
___06810-1	LONGARM AND THE INDIAN NATION #5	$2.25
___06950-7	LONGARM IN LINCOLN COUNTY #12	$2.25
___06070-4	LONGARM IN LEADVILLE #14	$1.95
___06155-7	LONGARM ON THE YELLOWSTONE #18	$1.95
___06951-5	LONGARM IN THE FOUR CORNERS #19	$2.25
___06628-1	LONGARM AND THE SHEEPHERDERS #21	$2.25
___07141-2	LONGARM AND THE GHOST DANCERS #22	$2.25
___07142-0	LONGARM AND THE TOWN TAMER #23	$2.25
___07363-6	LONGARM AND THE RAILROADERS #24	$2.25
___07066-1	LONGARM ON THE OLD MISSION TRAIL #25	$2.25
___06952-3	LONGARM AND THE DRAGON HUNTERS #26	$2.25
___07265-6	LONGARM AND THE RURALES #27	$2.25
___06629-X	LONGARM ON THE HUMBOLDT #28	$2.25
___07067-X	LONGARM ON THE BIG MUDDY #29	$2.25
___06581-1	LONGARM SOUTH OF THE GILA #30	$2.25
___06580-3	LONGARM IN NORTHFIELD #31	$2.25
___06582-X	LONGARM AND THE GOLDEN LADY #32	$2.25
___06583-8	LONGARM AND THE LAREDO LOOP #33	$2.25
___06584-6	LONGARM AND THE BOOT HILLERS #34	$2.25
___07727-5	LONGARM AND THE BLUE NORTHER #35	$2.50

Available at your local bookstore or return this form to:

JOVE
Book Mailing Service
P.O. Box 690, Rockville Centre, NY 11571

Please send me the titles checked above. I enclose _____ Include 75¢ for postage
and handling if one book is ordered; 25¢ per book for two or more not to exceed
$1.75. California, Illinois, New York and Tennessee residents please add sales tax.

NAME_____

ADDRESS_____

CITY_____STATE/ZIP_____

(allow six weeks for delivery.)   5

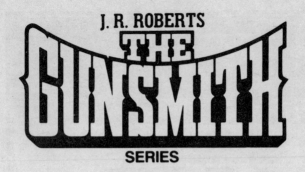

J. R. ROBERTS
THE GUNSMITH

SERIES